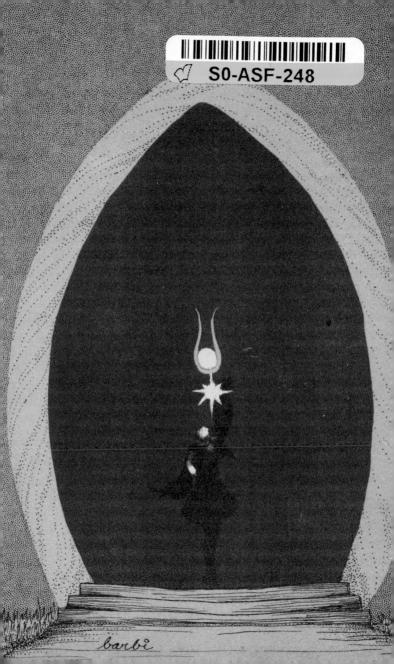

S0-ASF-248

barbi

FORERUNNER

Andre Norton

A TOM DOHERTY
ASSOCIATES BOOK

PINNACLE BOOKS
NEW YORK

FORERUNNER

A Tor Book.

First printing, May 1981
Third printing, May 1982
ISBN: 0-523-48558-1

PINNACLE BOOKS, INC.
1430 Broadway
New York, NY 10018

**Cover and interior illustration
by Barbi Johnson**

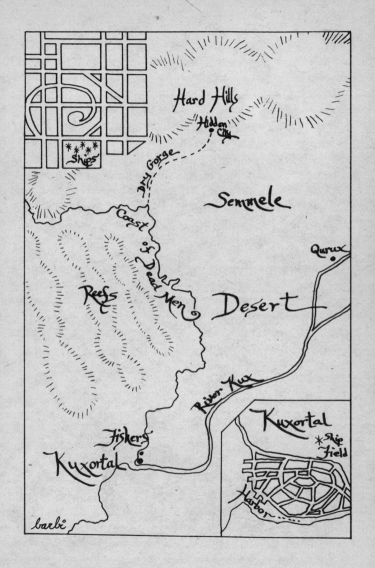

Hard Hills

Hidden City

Dry Gorge

Semmele

Ships

Coast of Dead Men

Qurux

Reefs

Desert

River Kux

Kuxortal

Ship Field

Fishers

Kuxortal

Harbor

barbi

FORERUNNER

barbi

1.

Kuxortal had always been—any trader would have sworn by his guild oath to that. No one had the need to dig deep into the mouldering wet-season, dry-season records (many layers of which had long since become dust, and dust of dust) to know that. The sprawling city stood on its own past, now well above the sea wharves and river landings, raised high on the mount of its own beginnings as men had tirelessly built on the ruins of other men's warehouses and dwellings, adding to the height of that mountain as the past leveled the holdings of their forebears.

The city had already been immeasurably old when the first needle ships of the space farers, those merchants of the stars who sewed together world upon world with their own trading ventures, had set down upon the plain beyond.

Kuxortal was old but it did not die. Its citizens had become an incredible mixture of races—sometimes of species—or mutations and new beginnings of life forms, springing out of old. Kuxortal had been favored ages ago by the fact that it had come to birth at the meeting of the river Kux (which drew upon the trade of a full continent, wafting boats and rafts to the western sea) with that same

baeli

sea. The harbor was a safe one even during the worst of the wet-season gales, its natural protections added to by the ingenuity of generations of men who knew all the perils of sea and wind, of gale and raider attack.

Once more it was favored when the star men came seeking not only trade but an open port where those who dealt in commodities which they dared not be subject to strict legal inspection might buy and sell in complete freedom—once the proper dues had been paid to the Guilds of the city. Now it had been well over tens of double seasons that rocket fire had scorched the plain beyond the town, and no one any longer marveled at the sight of an alien on the crooked streets which sometimes formed a deadly maze for the unwary.

For where there are traders and their riches, there are also predators. They also had their Guild, their standing in the hierarchy of Kuxortal, it being an old belief that if a man did not guard his own possessions, then he well deserved to lose them. Thus wily thieves and private guardsmen fought small secret battles, and the peacemen of the Guild kept safe by the rigor of their instant and bloody justice only those streets, those courtyarded homes, those trading depots which paid peace tax.

Just as there were thieves to prey upon the riches of Kuxortal, so were there also the small traders, those who lived like ver-rats in a grainery where there was no winged and clawed zorsal to go a-hunting, aided by dark-piercing eyesight. These, too, bought and sold, and perhaps some of them dreamed of making the big sale, the big find in the drift of strange merchandise, which would give them a chance to rise to greater profits.

Simsa was Burrow-wise enough not to dream big dreams—at least not enough to cloud the here and now.

She understood her very lowly place in the general scheme of life where she was near as small as a gamlin, and certainly as agile as those furred creatures who were used by the Lovers-of-the-dark in their own raiding parties. She had no people as kin—being, as she had known as far back as any child learns of the world about, one of those strange mixtures of blood and breed which added to the general difference of Kuxortal. Also knowing that her very strangeness made her vulnerable, and so disguising that strangeness as best she could.

She had been fetcher and errand runner for Ferwar—until the mists of the riverside burrow bit so far into Old One's crippled bones that her body at last gave up its spirit essence. Simsa it had been who dragged that light, twisted body down to the under holes and heaped over it there the cover stones. Ferwar had had no kin, and was somewhat shunned even by the Burrow dwellers, for she was learned in strange ways—some of which might be profitable, others hinting of danger.

That Simsa was blood kin to herself Ferwar had denied. However it was true that she never beat the child with her staff, much as she lashed out with an acid and biting tongue; also she passed on to Simsa much which would have surprised even a Guild Lord had one known where or what lived in the Burrows beneath his own palace-of-plenty.

The Burrowers were perhaps the least and lowliest of Kuxortal dwellers. They scooped out their dwellings from the mass of former buildings, sometimes being lucky enough to break into a cellar or a passage which could have been a long forgotten street, roofed over by buildings fallen during some raider assault before the dawn of time. Things could be found in Burrows, things worth trading, especially to the Star men, who seemed to take a perverse interest in broken bits which meant nothing to any denizen of Kuxortal. So such finds were close-held secrets and even among the Burrowers there were strongly defended treasure houses.

Simsa had her talents. Her agility had served her many times. Over and over she practiced ever with her lean body the twists, turns, and certain grips which Ferwar's hands, cramped even as they were by the painful crippling, had patiently shown her. As a Burrower she was small, though two seasons after the death of Ferwar she had suddenly shot up like a well-watered thrum vine. It was in that same season that she had changed her style of drab clothing, for Ferwar had been emphatic with certain warnings for the future. The loose smock she had always worn over breeches which had left her legs free for running and dodging, was not laid aside. However, under it she had wound a strip of stout chir cloth tightly about her body from waist up, constraining her breasts to give her still a childish flatness. That was a precaution she need only take with strangers—to those who know her, her own natural weapons made her untouchable.

Simsa's skin was black, a deep blueish black; in night darkness she could pad through any street which had no large number of lamps with a spirit's invisibility. On the other hand her hair, which she now wore confined and covered with another length of cloth, was pure silver light, as were her brows and lashes. Those she disguised with sooty fingers rubbed on a fire pot before she ventured out as she did, reveling in her ability to conceal herself.

She had her own form of steady livelihood, one begun when she had found a broken-winged zorsal fluttering out its life on a waterside rubbish heap—those mounds often provided unexpected finds for Ferwar. The zorsal had tried to bite—its sharp-edged jaws were strong enough to take a finger off a full grown man. Simsa had not stretched forth any hand at first, had only squatted down beside the injured creature, crooning to it in a small guttural sound which came from far down in her throat and which she had never made before; at that moment it had just come to her naturally as fit and right.

As the zorsal's first hissing and snapping subsided, and it settled down to watch her with huge, round, night seeing eyes, the girl had perceived that it was a female, its furred body heavy with young. Perhaps it had broken out of some warehouse cage, striving to find a place in freedom in which to nest and bear its coming brood.

Though Simsa had had no reason in her short life to trust or show any liking for another living creature (her bond with Ferwar being one of respect, awe and more than a little straight wariness) she sensed now within her a reaching out for another living thing which was perhaps as lost as she from any kin-tie. As she crooned, she at last advanced a hand, was able to touch finger tips to the soft down which covered the zorsal's back, felt even there the fast pound of the flyer's heart. After long moments the girl had been able to pick up the hurt creature, which nestled against her, giving Simsa a feeling such as she had never experienced before.

Zorsals were prized for ridding dwellings and storage places of larger vermin. She had seen them sold for solid sums in the markets and realized that she could now seek out the owner of this stray and perhaps claim a reward. Instead she took it back to the Burrow, where Ferwar looked at it but said nothing at all. Simsa, prepared to defend her actions, had been left oddly at a loss.

The zorsal littered within a night of her discovery of it.

She had bound up its injured wing as best she could, but feared that her tending was so awkward it might remain a cripple. Ferwar had drawn her aching body away from the mat place to watch the girl's struggle, finally grunting as she brought out of her jealously guarded supplies some salve which smelled oddly fresh and clean in a cave-room never touched by light of day.

There were two young males. Simsa had been right in her fear concerning the complete recovery of the mother. On the other hand the adult creature was surprisingly intelligent, in its own fashion, and after its cubs were weaned, it became Simsa's companion in her own night prowlings. Its eyesight was far keener than that of any human—even one trained as Simsa was, and it could communicate with a series of soft clicks which followed a pattern her own lips and throat could echo, so Simsa learned from it a small vocabulary of sounds which meant danger, hunger, others on the prowl, and the like.

In turn the zorsal trained its own young. Then Simsa, after a careful study of the market rented—did *not* sell—the two to Gathar, a warehouse commander who had dealings with the Burrower people from time to time, and was rated by them as never taking more than half of any profit. She paid her charges visits at regular intervals, not only checking on their care, but also continuing to impress upon them her own personality. When she went forth on most nights, the parent (whom she named Zass from a sound which it uttered when striving to attract her attention) rode on her shoulder, she having fitted a pad there as protection between the strong talons of the hunter and her own flesh.

Not only did Gathar pay her for the use of the zorsals (which, he admitted once in an unusual burst of good nature after a very successful bit of trading, were very well suited to their job), but also her regular trips to his establishment gave her a familiarity with another section of Kuxortal into which she could not normally have ventured while those on duty there grew used to seeing her come and go; after a season no one questioned her.

There were several among the Burrowers who had seen in Ferwar's death a chance to not only move into a snug and well situated lodging, but also marked Simsa down for bedmate . . . or profit. Traders from up-river—even some of the Guild Lords liked curiosities in women now and then. There were certain suggestions which she brushed brusquely aside. Then one day Baslter of the Hook decided to play no more with the whims of a female and strode up to establish ownership in a way he had twice before. A small crowd gathered to watch the fun. Simsa, standing straight before the entrance of her Burrow, heard the calling of small wagers back and forth.

She was so much the smaller and slighter, a child in their eyes, that the bettors found very few who would take their offered rates in her favor. Baslter drank heavily from one of the pots his followers handed him, swiped the back of his hair-furred hand across his blubber lips, and advanced as might one of the fabled Tall Ones from the inner mountains.

He was still out of reaching distance of the girl when she went into action so fleetly and with such driving force that her body appeared raised by a whirlwind, rather than through any action of her own.

As her feet lifted from the ground, her bare toes unsheathed to strike full against the man's protruding belly, raking deeply through even the leather of his jerkin. At the same time her body arched so that her hands struck the ground and, still raking upward with those claws, she somersaulted, rolled, and came lightly to her feet without more than a heavy intake of breath.

Baslter squalled. His hand going to the tatters of his jerkin came away red and wet. With the hook which gave him his second name he flailed out, prepared now to bury the metal in her flesh and jerk her close enough to crush the life from her with a single closing of his left fist upon her throat.

She was no longer there. As a zorsal might bait a pruhound, Simsa moved about the lumbering man. Not only did her toes unsheath those claws which few of the Burrowers had ever seen, but her outspread fingers carried equally grim and punishing armament. She sprang, tore, was gone, before Baslter, now bellowing his rage, could even turn to face the direction in which some agile bound had taken her.

At last, streaming blood, having yielded an eye to the punishment, the man was caught by several of his fellows and towed back and away, frothing in a fury which had no sanity left in it. Simsa did not even watch his retreat, but went back into the home she had so defended, there to sit down, shaking a little and fighting within her to control, first her rage, and then the deeper-seated fear from which that rage had sprung. Zass fluttered her good wing, made small movements with the crooked one, as at last, the girl conquered herself enough to take up a cloth, wipe her claws thoroughly, then, with a wrinkled nose, toss the rag into the basket which must be taken to the dump place.

Her victory over Baslter did not inflict her with overconfidence. She was well aware that there were many ways she could be entrapped by a man subtle enough of thought, and she did not underrate her neighbors on that score. It was then that Simsa realized the true worth of Zass and began to make very sure she was with her on every night foray, and installed a perch above the door of her Burrow where the zorsal could keep sentry duty when Simsa was within.

That the creature was also wary enough to protect herself the girl became aware on the day when Zass fluttered and hopped to her with a piece of meat, red, raw, of a nature to tempt the appetite. Simsa accepted the strip, examined it closely, discovering within a blueish mark which, she had no doubt, meant poison. It was from that hour that she began to think more constructively of her own future, of what she might do to climb out of the Burrows where she must now be ever on constant alert, not only for her own safety but for that of the creature she had come to value very highly.

Life in Kuxortal was layered in castes as well as by the mound of the city itself. A Burrower might lurk on the fringe of one of the least of the markets with his or her collection of salvaged bits and pieces, but such a meager trader could not even aspire to the smallest and most primitive of stalls. Thus most of their trading must be done either through the outlets of the Thieves' market, where they fared very badly indeed, or by trying to sell to a stall holder.

Since the coming of the sky men there had been a second market established, down by the edges of the fire-pocked field where their ships planted. But that was far too chancy to depend upon for any settled trading, since no one ever knew when one of the ships might arrive. Also, when it did the rush was so great that few—only the very lucky—were able to get near enough to one of the crewmen to even show his wares. They might not hope to trade for the cargoes of such ships, those were haggled over by the Guilds, but crewmen often could be coaxed into buying strange odds and ends, carrying out small ventures of their own.

Simsa had made a habit of hanging about and watching such transactions, and thus she knew that what the star men wanted most were curious things: old finds, or objects which were particular to this world, and small enough to be easily stowed in what must be very crowded and limited space on board those ships which had never been planned for the comfort of their crews, but rather to handle cargo valuable enough to make the long star flights profitable.

The cargoes they unloaded were varied also. Sometimes such simply rested in some warehouse, to be picked up again by another starship; in fact that was most often the case. Simsa, from what she had overheard, was very sure that much of it was Thieves' loot from a score of worlds—to be sold where it could not be traced.

On the hour Zass had brought her the poisoned meat and she knew that perhaps she would not even last over the few days left of the season unless she made plans which could outscheme Baslter and others of his ilk, (who now held her presence among them to be a personal affront), the girl turned out Ferwar's hidden treasures to examine them closely.

The old woman had had her own hiding places and most of those she had kept secret from Simsa also. But over the months since her death, with the aid of the zorsal's keen sight, the girl had managed to uncover a number of them.

Their burrow was one of those which had originally been a portion of a house, long buried by debris from above. Simsa had often marveled at patches of painting which still clung to the walls in one corner and had wondered what it must have been liked to have lived here when Kuxortal was lower and this house might have been even a portion of a High Lord's palace. The wall itself was of sturdy stones, set in careful pattern, yet not as solid as they looked.

Now she pressed at points here and there and then slid out what appeared to be intact stones, but were in truth shells of such, behind which were hollows from which she garnered all the contents, to spread these gleanings out on the floor and survey them critically to judge their market values.

Some that she knew or guessed might be of great value, though only to special buyers, she had to regretfully push aside, for Ferwar had collected old writings, pieces of stone on which were carvings of broken length, a few pieces of rotting leather scrolls which she had protected as best she could. Simsa could spell out some of those words, having been lectured on their value when Ferwar was in a good mood. Only none of them made sense. Now she bundled all those together and packed them carefully into a sack. Valuable to no one else, such just might be of interest to some starman, but she knew she had little chance of finding such a buyer. However, this was her day to check on her charges. If Gathar was in a good mood she could perhaps sell these to him at a price which might make her inwardly rage but would be more than she could raise by any effort of her own.

Placing the bag carefully to one side, she concentrated on the rest of the plunder she had uncovered. There was more hope of bargaining over this on her own.

These were the best of Ferwar's treasures, and the Old One had never told where she found them, but Simsa remembered seeing them from her earliest days, thus they had been a long time in the old woman's possession. The girl had often wondered why the Old One had not made some bargain—perhaps directly with Zack who was known to be a runner for the Thieves' Guild and who was as honest as any such would be (especially if first he were blood sworn as Ferwar could insist, and had in the past).

There were two pieces of jewelry, a broken chain of thick links of silver—bearing at one end a long, narrow plaque set with pale stones. The other was a thick cuff-like armlet certainly forged for the wearing of some man, also silver. It had a ragged break across it which destroyed part of an intricate pattern consisting of heads of outlandish monsters, most of which gaped wide to show fangs, those being insets of a crystalline, glittering stuff.

Both pieces came, Simsa was sure, from the far past. If she sold them to the wrong hands they would go for the metal alone, to be fed into some melting pot and so be forever lost. Something within her resisted the thought of that. She draped the necklet across her knee, and as she turned the armlet around in her hands, she thought.

There was one more thing—but that was her own find and she did not want to get rid of it. Also it had come to her almost as a gift from Ferwar, though she was not silly enough to believe in such things. When she had gathered the rocks to pile over that thin and wasted body she had seen a glint in the earth and scooped up what seemed to be a bit of metal, sticking it hurriedly in her belt pouch to be examined later.

Now she brought this out, laying the armlet aside. It was a ring—but not a broad band, gem set, such as she had seen commonly worn in the upper city. In its way it was cumbersomely made and awkward to wear. Still, as she slipped it now over her thumb (for that was the only finger it would fit) she eyed it with a fond feeling of possession. The band was fashioned of a silver metal which apparently neither age nor exposure could darken or erode. Its form, jutting well up above the round of her own dark flesh, was that of a towered building wrought with minute detail—showing even a tiny stair which led to a doorway in one of the two towers. The smaller of those towers had been used to form the setting for a white-gray opaque stone as its roof. There was a vague hint in its styling of one or two of the more imposing buildings of the upper hill. Still Simsa decided the ring was much older and of a time when there was much danger from raiders perhaps, and such structures were meant as positions of defense.

This was her own. It was not as beautiful as the other bits of jewelry, but something within her made her stare long each time she brought it forth. Sometimes a queer idea crossed her mind that if she were able to lift the milky jewel which formed that roof on the second tower and peer within she would see—what? Strange forms of life busy about their own concerns? No, not this to be sold, she decided quickly as she rewrapped and returned it to her pouch.

Even as she put out a hand for the bag of Ferwar's fragments with the plan of going straightaway to Gathar's, there was a roar. The ground under her shook slightly, small bits of broken stone and dust shifted from over her head.

A star ship had planeted.

Ferwar had spoken now and again of the luck which fate might dispose, even on those as lowly and portionless as the Burrow folk. Was this her luck arriving—so that on the very day, the moment when she had made up her mind to part with that which held the greatest worth, a ship had landed to offer her the best customers? She mumbled petitions to no gods, as some of those about her might. Ferwar had at times crouched over the fire basin, tossed a handful of larweed into the coals to puff out sweet smoke while chanting a sentence or two. However, the Old One had never explained to Simsa why she did so or what ancient power she might think would stir carelessly, if at all, to bring her an answer to such petition. Simsa had no gods, and trusted in no one—save herself, and Zass—and perhaps somewhat Zass's two offspring, who at least would answer her calls. But in herself first and most. If she were ever to achieve any rise above the Burrows, out of this constant state of having to be on guard, it would not be by the wave of any god's hand, it would be by her own determined efforts.

She slung the bag by its cord over one shoulder where the bones were sharply apparent, hissed gently at Zass, who made her crippled half flight down to perch on the girl's other shoulder. Then, after a quick look right and left at the opening of the Burrow, Simsa went out. It was still day, but she had taken the usual precaution of covering her hair and blacking her white brows. Her ragged clothing was drably brown-grey against the darkness of her skin, and, as she went down the zigzag path to where the river water washed, she passed very light-footed and as unseen as she could hope to be in daytime. Though she could not be sure that she would have no followers, the zorsal would warn her if any tried to overtake her.

One could not approach the landing field of the star ships too closely. All the town Guild officials would be there to greet the newcomer, their guards quick to drive off any save the representatives of those who had paid trader's tax and so wore their proper badges about their necks. Simsa could not go there as yet, but she could visit the warehouse which was her regular place of call each fifth day. No one watching her so far might guess she was planning to leave the Burrows for good.

Already her mind was busy with what she might do if she were able to part with the contents of the bag in the manner she wished. She would do the best bargaining possible, then go straight to the Thieves' market to dicker for clothing which did not stamp her as a Burrower. She had three bits of broken silver in her pouch, turned up on a last rake through of a side tunnel where she had been engaged in delving earlier. Those were worth something; even though they were but shapeless knobs of metal, that metal was not base.

Gathar was striding down the wide aisle of his main warehouse as she flitted in, keeping prudently to shadows as she always did. She had no need to call the zorsals. Through the dusk of the large building they came planing down to encircle her and their crippled mother, uttering sharp cries, their voices so high the girl could hardly distinguish them, though she had learned long ago that her hearing was keener than that of most of the Burrow people.

Their dam lifted her undamaged wing and fanned it, the leathery surface whispering through the air. At some signal from her which Simsa, for all her familiarity with the creatures, had never been able to catch, they went silent. The girl did not try her throat talk with them, rather padded on in a noiseless, barefooted tread until she rounded a mountain of crates to confront the ware-master himself.

He was in a good mood, showing teeth in a grin which suggested more a desire to devour than to please, but Simsa knew that of old. Now she made a single slight gesture with one hand — his eyes narrowed, were instantly drawn to the bag she shouldered. He pointed up the ramp which led to the quarters from which he could watch all the activity below. As Simsa ran lightly ahead of him, she heard his voice bellow an order or two before he followed. She was frowning, wondering just how much it would be worth to share a little of the truth with him. Their relationship had never developed any difficulties, but then she had always been the one with a necessary commodity to offer. Truth came very high in Kuxortal, sometimes beyond the power of any to buy.

As the bag thudded from her shoulder to the top of a table littered with sheets of tough grif-reed paper, all scrawled upon with untidy lines of crooked script, Simsa had her story fully in order.

"What's to do, Shadow?" Gathar asked. She saw, with satisfaction, that he closed the door behind him. So he thought that she might have something to offer worth serious notice.

"The Old One died. Some things she had worth selling to learned ones in the high towers. I have heard there are such who pore over such bits and pieces, just as mad about them as was the Old One. Look!" The girl opened her bag and dragged out several slabs of the inscribed stone.

"I don't deal in such." However, he came nearer, leaned over to peer at the markings.

"As we both know. But there is a profit in such, I have heard."

He was grinning again.

"Go to Lord Arfellen. He has taken a fancy these past two seasons to having men grub for such since that mad starman talked with him so long and then went off hunting a treasure which he never found. At least he never returned here with it."

Simsa shrugged. "Treasures are never lying easily about for one to pick up. The gateman at the High Place would never look or listen to a Burrower. I know that you shall take a goodly portion." She grinned in turn, her teeth so white in her black face as to startle one who did not know her. "But the Old One is dead—I have plans—I will give you these for fifty silver bits."

He exploded as she knew he would, but she also knew the signs—Gathar was caught. Perhaps he might use her bits and pieces to sweeten the temper of this lord he spoke of, gain some favor from him. That was the way Guild's men worked. They fell to serious bargaining then, and each was a worthy match for the other.

2.

Simsa turned this way and that, studying her reflection. The slab of cracked mirror wedged up on one end in the back of the frowzy tent gave one only a crooked view, but she nodded briskly in satisfaction at what she saw. The dealer in old clothes (undoubtedly many of her wares stolen) stood to one side so she could keep an eye on both the girl and the forepart of the tent which lay beyond the half division of a much mended curtain. Simsa strove to catch a glimpse of her back over one shoulder.

She had, she was very certain, chosen well, made the string of trade tokens, plus one of her bits of broken silver go farther than most she knew who dealt in this part of the market. Now she stooped and gathered up the smock and underpants she had discarded and rolled those into a bundle which she tied up into a shawl of a drab and dusty grey. The shawl she had insisted on sale-gift. It had a number of holes but it was still serviceable for transport purposes.

However, the girl who turned purposefully away from the cracked mirror was quite different from the ragged Burrower who had entered a short time earlier. Now she wore a pair of quasker-skin trousers tapered down to her slender ankles, their sturdy outer layer lined with softer

29

fes-silk. They were a dark, serviceable blue and perhaps had been snapped out of the luggage of some ill-fated land-rider. She was lucky in that they were so narrow of leg — a fact she had pointed out firmly to the seller. There were few potential customers who could have drawn them on with any ease.

Her own undershirt had been the best piece of clothing she had owned and she had kept it reasonably clean even in the Burrows. Simsa had a fastidious dislike of filth, and had washed both her underclothing and the body beneath it whenever she had a chance, a trait which most of the Burrowers found a matter of huge amusement. So this she had kept, and beneath it the band about her enlarging breasts; in its folds were hidden Ferwar's two jeweled treasures, plus the ring.

Over the chemise Simsa now wore the short coat of a courtyard upper servant. That was tightly sashed about her narrow waist, and she felt the weight of the long, wide sleeves which were gathered into wrist bands so that their folds also served as storage pockets. It was of the darkest color of the three Simsa had been offered, a wine, near black. There were roughened threads on one shoulder where some House badge must have been cut away, and it had no trim, except for a piping of silver gray about the high neck and wrist bands. The material was good; there was not a single mend nor fray, and the girl decided that it was enough to pass her into the lowest round of the hill city — perhaps even a round above that. Certainly she looked respectable enough to be allowed onto the ship-verge market, which was what she wanted now.

Her hair she still kept within its tight wrapping and she had darkened her eye lashes well before she had come into the market. Not for the first time she wished that nature had not made her so noticeable. Perhaps when she could make more free of the upper town she could discover some dye which would serve to keep her what Gathar had called her—a shadow.

"You are not the only buyer," snapped the woman by the curtain's edge. "Should you take all day to view those clothes you have stolen from me? Stolen indeed! I am too kind of heart with the young, too ready to give when I should get!"

Simsa laughed and the zorsal croaked.

"Marketwoman, when you are kind in any dealing the cie-wind of Kor will bring the vasarch trees into bloom. I should have bargained for a full turn of the sand glass longer, but I am in a good mood today, and you have profited by that."

The woman pursed her mouth in a gesture of spitting and made an obscene gesture. Simsa laughed again. She no longer had the bag she had left at the warehouse, but she swung the shawl bundle to her shoulder with the same practiced ease, then scooped up Zass who settled on her other shoulder. Slipping by the woman, she was out of the tent in a moment.

This section of the frowzy market was above the lines where the Burrowers were usually to be seen. For all of that the girl still kept a wary eye on what lay about her, the din of market seller cries and shouts being enough to cover the advance of an army.

By now the star ship would have landed, and the authorities should have begun dealings with the officers over the main cargo. There would be little or no trading with the crew until perhaps the next day. However, that delay would give the small traders, the lesser thieves, and the scavengers time to gather and stake out their own places, to wait until the crewmen were released for planet leave and a chance to dicker. Most of the crew would, she knew, from having watched a number of such landings during past seasons, head for the upper town, with its better drinking places where there were rent-women and other things denied during long voyages. Always, though, there were some to come seeking what they could buy—pickings which just might make them a small fortune when offered on another world. Simsa, shuffling sandals (which were a bit too large for her narrow feet, but in her present garb she could not go bare of sole) across the pavement, wondered briefly what it would be like to spend one's life going from world to world, always greeting the new and strange. She had never been away from Kuxortal, and, though she had explored all of the city save those crowning palaces at the very crest of the mound, her world was a small one indeed.

Those born in Kuxortal did not wander. They knew that there was a wide land behind them, a broad sea before. Ships came overseas, barges, smaller sailing, and slave-oared vessels down the river. Still the land immediately beyond the wide cultivated strips which provided the double croppings per year that fed the city was desert, and no man traveled on land when there was water of sea or river to carry him. There were a number of ancient and very strange tales about what might lie beyond the city gardens—tales such that no one was minded to prove the truth of them.

Simsa found a stall selling ripe fruit, some cakes of dark bread of nut-flour, and stacks of hardened packa pods hollowed out and filled with sap-sweetened water. Again she bargained, sharp-tongued and narrow-eyed, tucking her provisions into the ever-ready sleeve pockets.

As she prowled through the market, she eyed stalls and ground boards, assessing the worth of what she could see. Most here was broken trash but several of the dealers of such called a greeting as she paused, recognizing her for one who dealt in the lesser finds of the Burrowers. She knew that each and every one would note her new clothing, would speculate on how she had raised the price of such. Rumor spread through any market even faster than the first breezes of the wet season. She would be a fool to return to the Burrows now. There would be those who would lie in wait seeking to discover what she had found — what Ferwar must have treasured through the years.

The Old One had had her own ways of handling any upstarts who might question her rights. Only a cursing from Simsa, no matter how dramatically delivered, would mean nothing to the combined forces the Burrowers could assemble at the faintest hint of loot.

She went on down the long ramp which was only one of the many cut into the mound of the city, leading to the plain where the star ships planeted, twice backing against the wall to let pass trotting gangs of laborers from one warehouse or another, all of them wearing Guild badges on their grime-stiff sleeved jerkets, each group urged on by pairs of trumpet-throated bosses, one in the lead, one bringing up the rear. These would provide the transport for the off-laden goods.

There were others like herself, moving with purpose to find pitches at the ship field. A number led shaggy, hoofed beasts, horned and ugly of mood, from whose snapping teeth one kept a prudent distance, over the backs of which were hung bulging bags. These were the more important of that motley trading crew, and the majority of them went with a swagger, expecting all others, save of course the Guildsmen, to make way for them.

Simsa saw the ship clearly, looming near as high as the mound of Kuxortal itself, a gleaming arrow, finned down on still smoking earth where its landing rockets had scorched the ground, nose pointing arrogantly skyward. She had inspected a number of such during the past three trading seasons, drawn here by a curiosity she did not even try to understand. Though before she had had no chance to ever bespeak one of the starmen, nor sit in the fast crowding circles of those waiting small trades, where there were already squabbles, and, once or twice, a shouting and milling about of those waiting, as if they ringed in some fight.

Then the field guard came with a rush, striking out viciously with the peace staves against any in their general path. Thus all scattered quickly for there was no general law in Kuxortal; all men knew that a guard might lash out and club to death the unwary, and his action never be questioned.

She stood a little to one side of the general mass of waiting tradesmen. There were some who had already erected their four poled awnings and set up their boards. They were laying out their wares with the expectancy of those well accustomed to this game. Simsa could see that those flanked the way which was kept open for the passage of the cargo handlers—a passage which led directly to the side of the ship, a small section away from where there was already an open port ladder let out to touch the ground. Above was the cargo hatch, larger, also open, but nothing as far as she could see stirred within that. While on the ground at the forepart of the landing ladder gathered a knot of men wearing the uniform of star traders, conferring with several Guild masters—or else their First Men.

There was no way, she decided, that she could wedge into the already formed lines of temporary booths which walled in the alleyway right to the foot of the ramp. That was packed four and five deep with would-be merchants. Now she raised a hand and bit thoughtfully at the top of one finger, extending the claw to nibble at while she thought.

Zass shifted weight on her shoulder and uttered a very low, guttural noise. Zorsals were fond of neither the direct light of the sun nor crowded and noisy places. Simsa put up her hand to stroke her companion's furred head. The long, feathery edged antennae which served the creature for hearing and less understood sensing were curled tightly against its skull, and the girl knew without glancing around that its big eyes were nearly closed. Yet it was completely alert to all which went on.

Simsa reached the end of the ramp to wedge herself back to the rise of the city mound, her shoulders against its stone shoring of the mound face, watching intently as that group of men at the foot of the ship's ladder broke apart. Two returned into the ship, three others started along the open aisle toward where she stood, the Guild officers flanking them. None of the waiting small traders raised a voice to hawk any wares. They knew better than to attract the attention of the Guild; a market which was illegal but tolerated must avoid excess.

Simsa studied the star men as they came closer. Two of them wore what she had come to know as ship's uniform—their winged helms glittering in the sun, which also picked out the emblems appearing on collar and breast of their jackets. But the third of their party, though he wore a close fitting one-piece garment like their suits, as well as the boots of a star rover, was different.

His one-piece garb was of a silver-grey, not unlike the piping on her new coat, and he had no distinguishing badge. Nor did he wear the winged helm, but a tight fitting cap. His skin was not the dark brown of his companions but much lighter in shade, and he had dropped a step or two behind the rest of the party, who had completely ignored the would-be traders, his head turning from side to side as he went, as if he were fascinated by what he saw.

As he came up to the ramp Simsa studied him very carefully. It was very plain, she decided, that this was his first visit to Kuxortal, and, as a newcomer, he could be the very prey the merchants would be waiting for. It was difficult, of course, to judge ages—especially of these off world men—but she thought he was young. If that were true, then he must also be a person of some consequence or he would not be included in the party of Guild and ship's officers. Perhaps he was not part of the crew at all—rather some traveler who had been a passenger on board. Though why he would be here if he were no trader she could not begin to guess. His lighter skin was not the only difference about him. There was an oddity in the way his eyes were set and he was taller, thinner, than his companions.

Those eyes were never still, she also noted. Then they met hers—and held. She thought she saw a kind of surprise in them, he nearly stopped, as if he thought he had met her somewhere, sometime, and wanted to call a greeting. Her tongue swept over her lips as if she could taste the sweet drink which the Old One used only on state occasions. If she could but get to him now! That spark of interest he had shown in her was an opening for bargaining.

He must have rich resources or he could not be a star traveler. She shifted the sleeve in which hung the weight of those pieces she had retained, and was inwardly irritated that she dared not approach him now.

Only after having glanced so long and with such interest at her, he was now going on up the ramp. Zass gave another small cry, protesting the light, the heat, and the noise of the market. Simsa watched the stranger out of sight, her mind busy making and discarding a number of hopeful plans.

At length she decided that she could only leave matters to chance. The star man had noticed her where she stood. If he returned to the ship with any thought of individual trade in mind, then he might come seeking her. In the meantime there were others on board. Sooner or later they would be given planet leave—already the cargo crane had swung out of that larger hatch and the first of the boxes was swaying down to the waiting Guild handlers.

Simsa squatted down where she was, the mound to her back, the ramp close enough that she might have touched it—if her arm was only twice its length. She untied the shawl a little and Zass dropped thankfully down into the nest the girl so devised as she arranged the top folds to shelter the creature from the direct rays of the sun.

The girl was far away from the main lines of the merchants that none would try to encroach upon the small piece of ground where she so established herself, and she had learned patience long ago. It might be many turns of the sand glass before those from the ship would be free, which gave her time to fasten upon a plan of her own for attracting the right kind of attention. It was hot, and many of the merchants had settled down now, their wares ready; those who were fortunate enough to have a strip of cloth awning keeping well within it shade. As a Burrower she had long since learned to stifle discomfort herself.

Opening her packet of food she ate, sharing bites with Zass who was too sleepy to eat much and only wanted to be left alone. As she drank sparingly, Simsa's other hand sought within her coat for that packet of jewelry she had stowed in the safest keeping she knew. She had prudently kept two of the best picture fragments belonging to Ferwar. Those would be her come-on. Then, if she could judge the interest of any those attracted, she could produce the cuff armlet, which to her own valuing was the least important of her other wares.

The pieces of stone she brushed off with the edge of her sleeve and set out just beyond her knee near the ramp. One was the likeness of some kind of a winged creature, time worn so that only the general outline could be seen. The stone on which it had been engraved was a light green, veined with yellow—the veins having been cleverly used by the unknown artist to outline wings, and form a crest for the figure. Simsa had never seen such stone hereabouts, or even in the city. However, it might have traveled many days from the place where men had freed it from the earth and fashioned it to their fancy.

Beside it the other piece was in direct contrast for it was a velvety black, and it was not just a tracing upon a flat piece, but worked into the crouching form of an animal, with one paw upraised, claws spread—though several of those had been broken off. Only half of the head remained also and that was time worn so that one could see only a thick mane, the splintered stub of what must have been an ear, and a portion of face. For face it was, more than a beast's mask, having an eye, a nose, and a bit of mouth which was not too far different from her own.

The substance of the stone was somehow pleasant to the touch. Simsa discovered that rubbing fingers back and forth across it gave one the same feeling as one might have caressing finely woven material. This she had felt when she had been able to hold and finger lovingly a fragment of some rich fabric found among the rags the Old One had dealt in as long as she could still hobble about raiding the dumps and trash places of the upper town.

Now Simsa sat, rubbing her black stone, thinking and planning. Though now even her thoughts came more slowly; she had to make an effort not to drift into drowsiness. Even her long-cultivated patience was beginning to wear thin by late afternoon. The cargo had come out of the ship, been transported city-wards.

Along the way leading from ramp to ship, people were stirring, shifting their bits and pieces, hoping to catch the eye more quickly with this adjustment or that. Simsa stood up, moving about, loosening her legs from their cramped position. She could see the sky turning orange red and that worried her. If the crewmen did not come soon dusk would fall when they came and she would have no side lamp to show her wares. This would be a race between the setting of the sun and the ways of the starmen, a race which could disappoint her after all.

Zass poked her head from out of the bundle nest. The sensitive antennae on the furred head were half uncurled, an action which surprised the girl a little, for she would have believed that the subdued roar of the alerting market would have been too much for the zorsal. Now she noted that the creature's head had swung part way around so that it faced, not the line of merchants with the ship, but rather the ramp itself as that same small head was forced up and back to allow the creature as much seeing vantage in that direction as she could achieve. On impulse the girl swept Zass unceremoniously out of her bundle hiding place and brought the zorsal once more to perch on her shoulder.

Still the head was turned back and up towards the city, a certain intensity of that small body about which the wings were gathered like a night cloak developed as if she were about to be challenged. Yet Simsa could see nothing but the ramp, and, above its summit, the stir of guild guards.

Not for the first time she longed for clear communication with the creature. Though during the seasons she had nursed and sheltered the zorsal she had learned to judge much of the creature's emotions by its small actions, many times she could only guess. The zorsal now was nearly as alert as if she perched within striking distance of a ver-rat den and the den sharers were stirring, about to venture forth.

The girl clucked to the zorsal, drew the fingers of her right hand slowly and soothingly about the base of those half uncurled antennae. She could read no sign of alarm in the other's watchfulness, merely an alertness. Still that was enough to make her divide her own attention between the ramp and the star ship.

The cargo hatch was closed now. A light had snapped on, to glow outward from the smaller aperture which gave upon the landing stair. Below, the merchants were growing restless, there were noisy quarrels erupting here and there as they pushed and shoved for front line showing.

Finally there were crewmen coming out, Simsa counted five of them. They were too far away from her own place—badly chosen she now decided, and they seemed far more eager to reach the town above than to carry on any private trading ventures. In fact in their tightly fitted ships-clothing they had no pouches which showed that they transported anything of value. Also none carried a bag or bundle and they passed the calling traders on either side without so much as a glance at what they had to offer. Instead they ignored those, chattering among themselves and quickening pace towards the city ramp and whatever pleasures they had marked down for their own during a night of planet-side freedom.

Simsa fought down her disappointment. She had been very foolish to think that she might make the beginning of her fortune on the first such try. Certainly none of these looked to be the kind of man to pore over bits of broken carvings, and consider them worth a price no matter how small a price she might make it. She studied them carefully, however, as they brushed past the merchants, sometimes actually pushing some overly importunate man or woman out of their paths, talking in their sharp, clicking language which resembled at times a zorsal's grunts.

Nor did she raise her hand or voice to try to catch their attention as they strode past her chosen place to tramp up the ramp. Ruefully she stooped, picked up her pieces, drew out bits of rag to rewrap them. Tomorrow would be another day. Men long in space could well have other things on their minds this night beside trading, though that might be their whole way of life.

Here and there one of the disappointed merchants had already turned back to his or her pitch, set a brazier burning, getting ready a scrap meal. They would sleep curled among their wares, await the coming of sun and another contingent of star crew, or else these who had gone on their way back, their space starved appetites of the body sated, ready to think once more of long-term gain rather than fleeting pleasure.

Simsa hesitated over her own choice. She had promised herself that this night she would sleep in a real bed place in one of the taverns on the lower reaches of the street where carveneers sheltered during their stay in Kuxortal. Weighing her one sleeve was a twist of broken silver from which she could pinch a finger's length to ensure her that much. Also her position here by the ramp was not so choice a one that she need defend it by hunching there to sleep in the chill open.

She made her decision and started back up the ramp where the crew men, well ahead, were just entering into the town. The Guild guards glowered at her but there was no reason for any questioning. They did not police the field market, and unless she were one who wore a cheek brand of a failed, outlawed thief, or committed some act against the city peace right before their eyes, they could not cross weapons before her to take her for questioning. The neatness of her newly purchased clothes were those of one who could be a messenger for some House Merchant sent on a private errand where a house badge would be an advertisement her master was not prepared to allow.

"Gentle-homo—"

It had been one of Simsa's private employments to

learn what she could of other tongues. She could speak with the same fluency that she could mouth the Burrowers' coarse speech, the tongue of an upper riverman and two distinct seafaring dialects. Now she recognized off-world words—a salutation. But that it was addressed to her was a surprise which took her a breath or two to realize. It had been she who had been seeking to contact the starmen, she did not expect any of them to come seeking her. Nor was it one of the five who had climbed the ramp ahead of her, rather this was the stranger who come up town earlier with the officers.

He was looking straight at her though, and the Guild guards had taken several steps away as if to pay him deference. Now he pointed to the zorsal and said, haltingly, in the speech of the merchants of the upper town:

"You are the one Waremaster Gathar spoke of—the trainer of zorsals. I thought I would have to hunt far for you—yet here you have come as if I called and you heard."

Gathar, Simsa thought swiftly—why? Zass shifted on her shoulder and grunted. The zorsal's antennae had unrolled to the farthest extent which the girl had ever seen happen save when the creature was on night guard. Both of them pointed directly at the off-worlder as if the creature listened to more than Simsa heard, something other than those halting words.

"Will you give me of your time, dealer in old things—" the starman was continuing. "There are questions of import which mean very much to me—some of which you may be able to answer."

Simsa was wary. In her new clothing she was sure she looked more boy than woman, and she did not believe that this was some ceremonious route to name a bed-price. If Gathar had mentioned her in connection with old things . . . . Her fingers tightened about her swinging sleeve, weighted as it was with the two finds she had kept to tempt trade. All knew that the starmen were largely credulous about such discoveries and they could sometimes be bargained into such gains of trade as no one but the simple-witted here would strike hands over. She could not understand why Gathar had spoken of her at all. Which meant caution until she found out that much about *his* dealings. No one gave away even a smell of profit if he could help. However if this starman had come to her because of the Old One's bits and pieces she would make the best of what she had left. Now she nodded abruptly. Let him believe that she knew less of any save up town speech; such small precautions could sometimes lead to profit.

Taking her nod for assent he looked about over his shoulder and gestured towards the Street of Cull Winds leading off straightly to the left, down which the coming shadows crept out from several darkened patches between three or four welcoming door lamps of inns. It was not the best Kuxortal had to offer any traveler, still this was much better than the hostel she had thought to try. If nothing else she would gain a full belly out of this meeting; the starman could readily be maneuvered into paying for the food that he would offer out of courtesy before he would state his true reason for seeking her out.

3.

The room was low and dark. Along one wall well worn curtains hid a number of booths. Some flimsy lengths were drawn, and Simsa, in passing, heard the squeals of women, once the drunken brawling of a riverman's song. She stepped back to allow the starman to lead the way, her sense of caution fully aroused. On her shoulder Zass muzzled against her neck, thrusting snout right under her chin, antennae again curled close, as if the zorsal wanted a hiding place and was making do with the best she could find.

He who had brought them here swept aside a curtain to wave Simsa in. She chose a seat placing her back to the wall from which most of the room was in view. Involuntarily she flexed her claws a little, projecting their needle tips from her finger sheaths.

To the crop-headed boy in the stained shirt who lounged over to serve them she quickly gave her own order—making sure that she would not be fuddle-headed by any potion as strong as the traders used to bewilder those they would entangle in some ploy to bring themselves a double return. If starmen followed such practices she would be prepared.

This stranger might appear open-faced, even eager,

47

but a man could wear many masks and never show what lay beneath them. What still astonished her the most was that Gathar had spoken of her, and that in turn this one had recognized her from the waremaster's description. Unless, of course, it was because of Zass. She smoothed the head fur of the zorsal now. Only, this man had looked upon her down by the ramp when the zorsal had been hidden nearly from view. So— She waited for him to speak, knowing that thus a small advantage was hers.

He opened a large bag which had swung from his shoulder and which now rested on the stained table between them. From it he took with the same caution that one would use to handle leaf gold, two of the fragments she had traded to Gathar earlier that day. Seeing the care with which he touched those now, Simsa could have snarled in frustration. It was certain that Gathar had made an excellent bargain, far beyond what she had or could hope to gain herself. Under the table she felt again for the two things in her sleeve pocket and her hopes stirred higher. If such fragments were what this one sought for, she perhaps could drive her own price well higher than she had first planned.

"These—" the starman had laid his hand flat upon the larger of the two, "where were these found?"

He believed in coming directly to the point. Simsa felt a growing contempt triggered by this display of eagerness. Now she *could* believe that Gathar must have nicked him well if he had displayed the same eagerness to that trader old in well-learned craftiness.

"If you know Kuxortal," she answered, speaking slowly and with care, using the accent of the upper town, "you would also know that such as these," a flick of the finger pointed to what his hand near covered, "are apt to be found anywhere. Though—" (Should she pretend that such "treasures" were hard come by and that she alone held the secret? No, better not chance that; she had no idea what Gathar had told him already. Those she had sold were not the easily found gleanings of any dump, they were the result of seasons of delving first on Ferwar's part and then by Simsa herself.)

"You say anywhere—" he spoke slowly as she did, as one feeling his way through an alien tongue. "I do not think that is true. I have already spoken to Guild Lord Arfellen—" He was watching her narrow-eyed now, and Simsa sat very still, holding his stare with her own eyes, determined not to let him see that he made any impression on her, if he had meant that as an implied threat. He could, with fewer words that he had just mouthed, have her up into the question room of a guild and that was something to shake anyone's mind with fear.

Zass quivered until the girl could feel the shaking of the small body so close pressed against her. The zorsal was always, she had discovered long ago, well able to pick up her emotions, translate them in turn into a reaction of the creature's own. The girl stroked the leather wings covering the upper part of the back, unable to see how she would twist and turn to answer with anything but the truth.

"Those I did not find—not all of them." Truth had a bitter taste when it was forced out of one and she seldom had used it save with Ferwar, who had always recognized a lie and could not be misled.

"The Old One died—what she had saved was then mine. She sought old things and dreamed over them, believing them true treasures."

He did not answer her at once, then the serving boy was

back with their footed drinking horns, two platters of still smoking stew, tongs and spoon stuffed upward in the center holders. The starman had swept his finds off the table, into his bag, and out of sight, with a swift deftness which Simsa was forced to approve. It would seem that, if he was willing to show her what he carried, he had no mind to let others inspect such wares.

Zass stirred and scrambled down from Simsa's shoulder quickly. Such a lavish display of food was not common for either of them and the zorsal could be greedy when she had gone on short rations for a day. The girl picked up the tongs, searched for a lump of meat as big as her thumb and proferred it to the creature who seized eagerly with a throaty gurgle.

"The small one," the starman observed, "seems well trained."

Simsa chewed and swallowed a fragment of crisp tac root, spicy from being broiled in the stew, before she answered:

"One does not train zorsals . . . ."

Now she saw him smile and his smooth face looked even younger. "So we have been told many times over," he agreed. "Still it would seem that this one lives content with you, gentlehomo. While Gathar admits that he has never had better hunters of vermin than those he received from your hands. Perhaps only you have the secrets of the art to make friends between man and such."

Was he trying flattery now? There was no reason for him to believe that she could be so moved to his will. He must have sensed her instant wariness, or read it somehow in her face, for he had laid aside his own tongs and spoon, making no headway with his stew, but took up his drinking horn and watched her across the rim of it, as he sat with it half way to his lips, a picture of a man caught up in a puzzle.

"Your Old One—she was a Burrower." He did not make that a question but a statement and Simsa knew that he must have gotten from Gathar all the waremaster knew. "Did she find many such in burrowing?"

Say 'yes' Simsa decided quickly and she might unleash on the Burrows half a force of guild men. The same would be well warmed with anger when they found that there were no such pickings left. She must be very careful.

"I do not know where first she found such." That *was* the truth. "Of late she traded for them—"

The starman leaned forward, setting down his drink as untasted as his dinner.

"With whom did she trade?" His voice was low, but he rapped that out with a ring of authority which again hinted of the power to discover what he wished to know if he need call on such aid.

"There was—" More truth, enough to lead him away from her, point him toward the source which had dried up a good four seasons back and the uncovering of which would reveal nothing now, "one of the rivermen who was in debt to the Old One. From time to time, he brought such, then ceased to come—death is easy along the waters and he was said to be a man with a price on him—a thief who had broken faith with the Master."

Though those oddly shaped lids veiled the starman's eyes, they had not moved quickly enough, she had seen that sparking of interest there. So telling the truth was the right path here after all. Turn this one's nose up river and she was free of him.

The heavy downward swing of her sleeve was a reminder of what she still carried. Why not make a deal with him since he was a hunter of old things? He believed her story, of that she was sure, and, since he was so eager, she could get enough for them. Quickly Simsa disciplined her soaring hopes, it was never well to tempt fortune by expecting too much.

Now she pushed aside the platter before her and moved to unfasten the tight wrist band of her sleeve. Not the jewelry; those she would hold on to until the last. But the other things.

She reached inside the inner pocket and pulled out the broken beast carving. He was looking at them now as if *they* were the plate of stew and he was a Burrower who had gone at least a day and a half without eating.

"These are the last!" She was determined to make that plain. "I would bargain for them."

He picked up the carved beast before she could stop him. Turning it about as if it were the most precious possession of a Guild Lord.

"X-Arth— It is X-Arth!" His voice was hardly above a whisper and the name meant nothing to her. But her hand shot out to cover the piece even as he tried to raise it closer to his eyes.

"First we bargain," Simsa said firmly, taking the opportunity to sweep with her other hand, bringing the second piece of stone under her palm. "First—what is X-Arth?" She might well sell these two bits if the starman met her price, which she had revised upward several times in the space of the same number of breaths. However it would be well to know *why* these, or at least the one piece, was so important. All such knowledge which could be filed away in one's head made one just that more able to keep life in one's body.

He put the piece down very reluctantly, releasing his

hold on it so she gathered it in.

"It means 'out of arth'—from another world—a very old world on which, some believe, all our kind originated. Or at least some of us who range the stars believe it. Tell me, have you heard of an off-worlder—a man named Thom T'seng?"

"The crazy witling who went up river and then into the desert about the Hard Hills? He went hunting treasure, but he never returned. Men do not spit in the face of luck by journeying so."

"He was my elder brother." If the starman had resented her contemptuous estimate of his close kin-blood's mentality he gave no sign of it. "It was another kind of treasure which he sought, knowledge. And he had good reason to believe that he could find it. This—" he touched finger tip to the head of the image, "would argue that he was right. I have come to try to find him."

Simsa shrugged. "If a man puts a knife to his throat and says 'I would let out my life', why stop him? The world is over-full already of fools and turned-wits," she repeated words of the Burrows. "Some live, some die, some seek death, others flee it—it is all the same in the end."

His face was expressionless now. "Fifty mil-credits."

Simsa shook her head. "I do not deal with off-world payments," she answered decisively. Zass reached a long thin limb across her arm and clawed up a lump of stew for herself. The girl did not care. Her own hunger was not assuaged, but she was uneasy. If this off-worlder knew or guessed, he could take those two bits which he wanted so much and have her thrown out, hunted down slope, perhaps beaten into a broken-boned pulp by merely raising the cry of "Burrower" in this upper city place.

Also, if she tried later to get rid of off-world payment in any money changer's stall she could condemn herself as an unregistered thief. Now she was well able to see the folly of having come here at all—she was the witling!"

"I will pay the credits to Gathar, he will change them for you."

Simsa bared her teeth in just such a snarl as Zass could show when she was crossed. Use the waremaster man for a cross-payer? What did this off-worlder think she was? She would be lucky to get two tens of anything he left for her by doing so.

"Pay me ten tens of loft marks, in broken silver," she returned, "and no less."

"So be it!" He held out his hand palm down above the two old pieces. The move awoke her complete amazement. For a moment she regretted not having demanded twice as much. Still, caution advised her quickly, it is never well to be too greedy. For one ten of broken bits she could establish herself in the lower part of the upper town, find some way to earn her living well away from the Burrows. If the starman did not know how to bargain, then she was the winner.

Simsa swept both of the pieces back into her sleeve pocket and snapped shut the wrist fastening. Then she dropped her hand across the waiting palm to seal the bargain between them, her skin looking so dark against that of the off-worlder.

"Bring me the silver and both are yours—the bargain is set and may fortune strike us both with her dark wand if we fail in it!" She recited the old market place formula which even a thief would not gainsay once it passed his lips.

"Come with me to Gathar's and I'll have it in your

hands now."

Simsa shook her head determinedly. To have such a piece of good fortune viewed by even a half-friend was stupid. Only what if he told Gathar why he wanted such a sum? That would be as bad for her as having it paid right under the other's eyes. How much did she dare explain to this stranger? Could she depend on any understanding from him at all?

She had thought herself so clever, her plans had appeared so smooth in anticipation—why had she not foreseen these difficulties? She surveyed that smooth face, those strange half-hidden eyes. Then she looked directly at the zorsal and with tongue against teeth made an odd, clicking noise.

Zass had finished the piece of meat she had snatched, her thin purple tongue darted into first one corner of her big mouth and then over to the other. At Simsa's signal she raised her head with a jerk, her antennae uncurled and rose straight up, the fine feathery hairs along the edges quivered.

"Put out your finger!" the girl commanded, making a gesture to the zorsal. The off-worlder look at her for a long moment and then obeyed.

The creature's long neck stretched, her pointed snout, ringed round with fangs, two of which were hollow and filled with a poison which could make a man suffer for hours, approached that finger. Then the antennae flicked down, the tip-ends just touching hand and finger for a second.

Zass turned her head on her hunched shoulders, made a guttural sound. Simsa drew a deep breath. This was a new thing between them and it had been used only two or three times before—each time proving that Zass was right in her estimation of the good or ill will of those so tested. There was still the fact that this was an off-worlder and so some strangeness in him might not register properly for the zorsal, but as far as Simsa could now see she had very little choice anyway. She could only protect herself in so much.

"Do not tell Gathar of me, or of why you want the silver. Get large pieces, not broken bits from him, and say that you could not find me. Exchange then the takals for bits. Then bring them to—" Not to the Burrow—she had no intention of returning there ever if she could help it. But earlier, after she had put on her new clothing, she had done some scouting of the inns in the lower regions and had marked down one she had thought might serve her purpose—The Spindwaker. It sheltered river traders but this was not the season when it would be crowded, and it had a reputation for not encouraging brawling, also the Wifekeeper there paid her dues regularly to the Thieves' Guild and those within its walls were safe from pilfering. Swiftly Simsa told the off-worlder of the place and how to find it.

"What do you fear?" he asked quietly when she had done.

"Fear? Enough of everyone and everything to make as sure as possible I keep breath in my body," she told him sharply. "This world teaches one sharp lessons: learn or die. I shall expect you before the dawn gong—will that be so?"

"As close to that as I can make it," he agreed.

Simsa slid out of the booth, scooping the zorsal up as she went. The sooner she was undercover in her proposed shelter for the night the better. Though in the streets, now dusk filled, she could depend upon the zorsal to give alarm of any who might follow either to spy or to rob.

When she leaned against the half opened shutter of the cubby in the inn she was torn between walking, or rather stealing forth, from her present room, or waiting for the dawn gong and the off-worlder. Simsa had no liking for such risks as she believed she might be running now. She could watch the street below for a goodly length in both directions, while the zorsal perched on the edge of the shutter itself, its head bent at what might appear an impossible angle, gazing with the same intentness, and, the girl knew, far better night sight.

There was an over-abundance of shadows along the way. Here in the lower town the lamps were well apart both for reasons of economy and the desires of those both dwelling and walking here after night fall. She had marked carefully the comings and goings of a few. But she was sure that perhaps others made far less visible journeys which she was not aware, for the zorsal had picked up at least three such.

Since there was no reason for the off-worlder to come with any great stealth she did not allow herself to do more than catch a quick breath or two at the quivering of Zass's extended antennae and try to judge, by the movements of those slender wands, who passed. She thought once she caught a shadow but that was all.

In her room she had blown out the lamp as soon as the frowsy maid had left. Then, with Zass's small grunts as a guide, had explored it with care, learning its dimensions by feel and an odd impression of proximity which she had learned during her working with the creature now riding on her shoulder.

Though she could not in all earnestness say why she felt so uneasy, it was like a warning of trouble to come, and against any such Simsa prepared in her own way. She had made three circuits of the small room, the first slow and tentative, the last with the sureness of one walking a well known path. After each she paused for some time to watch out of the window.

The off-worlder had offered what was to her a fabulous price. His eagerness without the process of bargaining made her suspect he might have given even more. But greediness itself was a threat, and one she would not bring down upon herself. She still had the jewels, too. The Old One's treasure was a goodly inheritance indeed.

There was someone coming, walking plainly down the middle of the narrow, cobble-paved street. He came with confidence and as he passed beneath the light of the second lamp from the first corner, Simsa identified the fitted body-suit of a starman.

Only—

Zass's antennae stiffened, the zorsal rumbled a low note of warning. As the starman came on Simsa pushed the closer to the window, knowing well that her dark face, from which she had not rubbed the soot that overlaid her brows and lashes, could not be sighted by any watcher below.

Six paces such as his long legs would take, a little more, from the outer door of the Spindwaker's, and a shadow detached itself from another doorway diagonally across the way. With a leap like that of a throat-slashing ver-rat the lurker was on the man she waited for, hurling feet inward in one of those maneuvers practiced by night runners, so that boots, especially made for the purpose with four heavy thicknesses of hide, would strike against the back of the intended victim's legs, sending him forward in a helpless crack against the cobbles.

Thus the attacker planned. Only, when he would have thudded home, to complete his skillful and long practiced attack, this victim had moved with a matching speed slightly to the left. Only one of those boots struck, as at the same time, the off-worlder spun about and brought a hand chopping down.

Simsa's hand struck out into the night air in turn, without her quite realizing that she did so (unless she could not bear to so easily lose the only fortune she had ever come even promise-close to obtaining). Zass, though her flying skill had never been restored since her wing had mended, was still not altogether lost in the air. The zorsal's claws scraped the girl's arm as she ran down its length, Simsa holding steady until the creature took off in a fluttering downward spiral which was far from the beautiful, exact swoops of her progeny, but which landed her near upon the struggling men below. Simsa turned and grabbed for a weapon—the extinguished lamp on the table. Pushing that, dripping its oil down her, into her broad girdle, she flung the shutter wide and followed the zorsal out.

There was a narrow ledge, which she had earlier marked, running to the edge of the inn's front wall. From that it was easy enough to swing to the pavement, land with the expertise she had learned years earlier. Once she had shaken off the jar of her meeting with the cobbles, she was on her feet and running.

There came a screech from the entanglement on the pavement. Simsa nodded to herself. As silent as any night thief, the unexpected attack of a zorsal was something which could tear worse than that cry out of him if Zass was given a fair opening to go for throat, face or eyes.

Before the girl reached the fighters they had separated.

One lay in a huddle on the ground, but the one who had risen to his feet was clearly the off-worlder. There were voices now—Simsa reached the two and the man turned, crouching, ready to attack just as she got out:

"Come, star rover!" She caught at the arm which was rising to aim at her, held on while she stooped and dropped her heavy burdened sleeve for the zorsal to catch at and climb so swifly that its claws tore well into even that stout material.

Then with her fingers sliding down the man's arm to close about his wrist, she jerked him towards the other end of the street.

"We run!" she said and gave an extra pull to the wrist she held as a way or urging him on.

He did not stop to question her, and for that she was thankful, as, still hand linked, they dodged into a side street, found the wide door of the inn's ware entrance and that gave to the nudging of her shoulder. Since there were no rivermen here to leave their cargoes in the cubbys provided, she had made very sure earlier that the bar was loosened to aid in an unseen going or coming. The Burrowers' instinct that one must always have two entrances at least to every hole had brought her to make this discovery and prepare to take advantage of it.

Inside she led her companion up the back stairs to the upper roofed but unsided gallery and so through a hall and into the room. Even as she dropped the bar of that into place, and was free to jerk the dripping lamp out and smack it down on the uncertainly legged table, she could hear movement, low voices, and a clatter in the street.

The zorsal fluttered toward the now open window where Simsa, brushing past the off-worlder, was also a moment later.

There were men below—at least three of them—gathered around one who lay groaning on the pavement. Coming with stick lamps down the street were peacemen—who never ordinarily ventured into this district at all. Simsa's eyes narrowed almost as did Zass' when the sun struck them. There was no reason for the Guild Watch to come—who had summoned them? The one cry the assailant had uttered could not have reached over five streets, up one wide avenue, to their usual patrol route. Even if it had they would have taken no note, since that sounded from the lower town. The Thieves' Guild had their own watchmen—so—

"Arfellen's men—" He spoke in a whisper which was uttered so close to her that his breath could be felt against her cheek. She started, unaware that he could move so silently as to come up beside her without her noting.

Lord Arfellen! So sure was she that the attacker had been one of the Thieves' Guild that at first the name he had uttered meant nothing to her. Then she saw in the blaze of the stick torches gathered in a knot about the man still lying on the pavement (some of those about him had managed to get away before the arrival of the watch guard, but two were having their arms twisted expertly behind their backs, nooses drooped over their heads) that these same guards wore shoulder badges not of the Guild itself but of some lord's personal following—

Arfellen! Without thought Simsa whirled, her claws unsheathed, ready to tear to ribbons this fool who had brought down up her such disaster. She heard her own guttural sound of sheer rage, not unlike that cry of Zass's when the zorsal was about to attack. Her claw nails caught—once—and then there was a grip of iron about her thin wrist; expert in defense as she was, she could not break that grasp. He twisted her arm about and up behind her shoulders with the same ease that the guard below made sure of their prisoners. Next he would march her down the stair, join her to that sorry company and what she could expect waited beyond!

Simsa shivered, and hated herself for shivering. However, instead of jerking her around and pushing her towards the door she had so lately barred, he instead pulled her closer to him. His other arm came up about her waist holding her a vise of bone of flesh strength such as she had never met before, once more then he whispered, his breath once more warm against her cheek.

"Be still!"

Completely bewildered, Simsa tried to understand. Was the starman not going to claim protection from one of the foremost and most powerful guild lords? Surely that squad below who had come so swiftly after the attack on him must have been sent for his benefit. It was well known that the off-worlders were not to be touched in Kuxortal—they were not to be considered natural prey by anyone, high or low.

Yet this one did not call down to his would-be deliverers. He was acting instead as might a man who had something to hide, or someone to fear. Slowly Simsa relaxed a little, no longer tensing her whole body against his prisoning hold.

4.

No one approached the inn door nor the doors of any of the other buildings though Simsa fully expected them to come searching for this off-worlder. Why else would the personal guard of one of the highest of the Guild Lords trail him to this lower level? She stood unresisting now in his grasp watching the men gather up the one lying on the street, forcing at least two of their other captives to carry him, or rather half drag his limp body between them, as the whole party started up slope the city above.

Zass had flown over to hang on the shutter, her antennae fully extending towards what was happening below. Now, as the guards went on their way, the off-worlder released the girl and reached out to swing the shutters to, leaving them in darkness.

"What do you do here?" Simsa broke the silence of that darkness first. She had to know what he was involved in in order to prepare for her own defense.

"What I promised—to bring you this!"

She heard a rustle in the dark, then a clinking from where the table must stand.

"Here is the reckoning between us."

She felt her way to the table, sought the lamp. A

goodly portion of its content had gone on her when she had seized it up as a possible weapon. She stank of its thick odor. Now she clicked a fire-spark and set what was left to its work. There was indeed a pouch, a fat pouch, on the table top. On the other side of the board stood the off-worlder watching her through eyes which seemed now to be the narrowest of slits.

Simsa made no move to touch the pouch. To be drawn further into this stranger's affairs, even just to the point of selling him what he wanted, was the last thing she desired. Yet—they had made trade bargain—and no one save he, she, and the Old One (in her time) knew of the two pieces Simsa carried. She was very certain that if they did trace what she had sold Gathar back to her, they could not fix on this second sale. She would leave here before dawn, using that same back way—or even the house tops if she must. Still—she had to know.

She used her oil sticky fingers to free the wrist band of her sleeve, seek out the carvings, not looking at what she did, rather keeping a wary eye on the other. He had not moved and his hands, free and empty, hung in plain sight.

As the girl pulled out the small packet which contained the carvings something else spun free into the light of the lamp, the violence of its spin freeing it from the scrap of cloth she had thought so firmly bound around it. It was as if fate itself had begun to betray her, Simsa thought, as she snatched for that, caught only the cloth and dumped the contents fully into the shine of the lamp.

The ring did not glitter, the metal of its fashioning was too soft a sheen, it had been buried perhaps too long, and its single remaining stone was milkily opaque and not cut to blaze forth in glory. Yet there was no mistaking, no hiding now what had so seemingly loosened itself through no will of hers.

That circlet with its tiny castle mount for the unknown stone lay revealed to both of them. Simsa hurled aside the packet of the carvings, scooped, with claw-extended fingers, for the ring. She might have parted, had there been both opportunity and need, with the two other pieces of jewelry—those from the Old One's caches, but this—no! From the first moment she had found it something within her claimed it, knew that it must be hers alone.

Though the off-worlder had picked up the packet, shaken the carvings free of their covering and inspected them as any prudent purchaser would, he quickly turned his attention again to her hand. For some reason, perhaps defiance, because he had handled her so easily at the window, Simsa did not thrust the ring into hiding once again. Rather she slipped it over her thumb in full sight.

He did not bend his head any closer to view it. Still she was as certain as if he did, that he studied it with care. Then, at last, he said—as if the words were forced from him against his will:

"And from where came that?"

"This?" She tapped it with the slightly extended foreclaw of her other hand. "This was the Old One's gift—(which was truth after a fashion—had Simsa not labored to bury Ferwar she would never have chanced on it)—I do not know from where she had it."

Now he did extend his hand. "Will you let me see it?"

She would not take it off, the longer she felt its weight on her finger the more natural that seemed. But she lifted her hand a fraction closer to him.

"X-Arth maybe," he said very softly, almost in wonder.

"The ring could be that of a Moon Sister, or High Lady. But here?" He must ask the question of himself rather than her, Simsa decided. She had a new flow of curiosity.

"What is Moon Sister? A High Lady? Yes, of them I have heard."

He shook his head and there was impatience in his voice when he answered.

"I do not speak of the Lady of one of your Guild Lords. The High Lady was of another world and time. She could summon powers my race were never able to measure, and the Moon was her crown and her strength."

Though the Burrowers gave no lip service nor bowed no knees except to Fortune, Simsa thought she understood: A goddess.

The temples of the upper city served only those with precious metal to pay for sacrifices (not that Simsa had ever heard of any surprising answer to prayer muttered or full-sung in any of *those* halls). If there were gods and goddesses on this world they busied themselves only with those who already had the warm right hand of fortune on their shoulders. Only how did the symbol of a goddess known to the off-worlder come to lie under a rock down by the burial pits?

This X-Arth he hunted—what did the Lord Arfellen have to do with that?

"Those guards—they followed you." She flipped the ring about so only the band was showing, the castle, as he called it, lay against her palm in hiding. "What has Lord Arfellen to do with you—or—what is more important—does he know of me?"

She was not sure he would tell her. He was frowning now, wrapping the carvings in the same piece of cloth she had used, putting them with care into his belt pouch. He did not answer, but rather went once more, with a tread so quick and easy that in spite of his spacer's boots he made no sound crossing the room, to peer out a crack between the shutter and the casing.

"The lamp—" He made an impatient gesture and she guessed what he wanted, blew out the flame, then heard the squeak of the shutter as he must have pulled it farther open. Zass complained with a growl and Simsa joined the off-worlder in time to take the weight of the zorsal back on her shoulder.

There was nothing below. No one moved. They might be looking down upon the street of a deserted city. Simsa, bred to the Burrows and the alarms of the fringe places, understood the threat which hung as a part of that very silence.

"Lord Arfellen—" she whispered.

He made a swift movement, held his hand hard across her mouth. His answer came in the thinnest thread of a whisper. She wouldn't have believed he could have spoken so softly and yet have the words reach her with such clarity.

"Listen well—Arfellen's men followed me to spy. Is there any way out of here? He may have loosed more than just the guard to dog me—"

How much would her help be worth, that question flashed first into her mind, only to be followed by the sense of her own danger. If the Guild Lord's men hunted this off-worlder, an alien whom all the customs of Kuxortal protected, then how much more they would profit in taking her for whose very skin they would not have to answer to anyone? They could crush her dry in one of their question rooms and learn all she knew—yet try to wring more out of her. Only if the off-worlder was safe—for now—could she also hope to have time to work out her own method of escape from his troubles.

There was only one place—the Burrows. No one of the upper city came seeking there. There were far too many runways and passages, too many hiding holes. Those from the upper city had long ago given up hope of flushing any who fled there, depending indeed on the clannishness of the Burrowers themselves, who resented any newcomers and would set up and deliver up to the authorities an upper town fugitive.

Only if one struck a bargain with a Burrower—one of enough weight of arm to defend himself and his prey—could any fugitive hope for refuge—then only for a short time.

Simsa's thought spun back and forth in a whirl. There was one way she could take the off-worlder back to the very den she had hoped to have seen the last of. It would cause talk, yes—but she could do it openly and none would stand between her and a dubious, fleeting safety. First—the money.

She pulled out of the off-worlder's loose hold to catch up the bag of broken bits, stuff it deep into her sleeve and fasten the wrist button. Then her hands went to the tight wrapping about her head. She pulled off the many strands of that, shook free her thick matt of silver hair, then smeared the band pieces across her eyebrows and lashes to remove some of the protective coloring. She was not to be Shadow now, but play a very different role.

"There is a way," she said softly as she scrubbed away her disguise. "We have some play-women in the Burrows. None have ever brought back a ship man. Though some of the lesser river traders—when they are drunk enough—will come for their pleasure. Take this," she groped her way to the bed she had hoped to lie soft on and never had a chance to even try, and snatched up its upper cover, pushing it on him where he stood a darkened blotch between her and the open window, the lights from below giving her that much guidance now. "Put it about you as a cloak. Now—if you can stand being thought a Burrow woman's pleasure buyer!"

He was following her, though she was not sure at that moment whether she wanted that or not. Once more they made the way through the back parts of the inn, even as they had entered a short time before.

As they came under a dim lantern she thought she heard a faint exclamation out of him, but when she turned her head quickly he was quiet. So they passed into a side street, Simsa in the lead, he following with that soft tread on her very heels. Down they went, skirting a wall which was a division point between the city and the fringe. There were secrets there, known well to her people. She stopped beside what looked to be a regular section of that same wall, but was merely lamperwood, hard as iron even in such a small panel and skillfully overlaid with paint and dirt to appear as solid as the stone on either side.

Simsa slipped through that easily enough, her large companion found it a tighter squeeze, but he did not delay her longer. She went only a few more steps until she darted into a cellar left open to the sky and then caught his hand to lead him through a maze of passages far better known to her than the streets above their heads.

Thus she came back after a momentous day and night in a full circle to that place she had never thought to see again—Ferwar's Burrow. In the dark she found a battered lamp which fed upon not oil from the upper city but the squeezings of certain ill smelling ground nuts which had to be pressed for weary spaces of time to give forth their juices, so that lamp light at all was treasure in the Burrows. Still if there were eyes for the seeing now, let them mark that she was not alone.

However, as she set spark to the battered saucer-like bowl of mud which held that oil she was not prepared for the wonderment in the off-worlder's eyes. For a moment she was startled at the strange look he turned upon her. Then she remembered that for the first time in years she had taken off that discreet covering which had made her "Shadow."

"But you are—you are a woman!" His surprise was so open and complete that she was startled a little in turn. Did her disguise then hold so well that even her sex had been undiscovered when she ventured forth? He had indeed, she remembered back now, addressed her by that queer off-planet greeting she had heard given to males. But she had merely thought that these aliens had but one form of greeting for all.

Now, hardly knowing why, she raised her hands and ran her fingers through her silvery hair. It floated a little at the touch, the electricity aroused by her treatment moving its lighter strands. It was seldom and only in private nowadays that she unwrapped her hair so. In fact now she felt an odd kind of embarrassment which was better left hidden.

"I am Simsa—" Perhaps Gathar had already spoken her name.

She saw the look of awe change into a slight smile on the off-worlder's face.

"My House name is Thom," he placed his two hands together, palm meeting and bowed across them. "My given-by-father name, Chan-li. My friend name—Yun."

Simsa laughed suddenly. "What a world of names! How do those you know choose among them if they would call you?" She seated herself cross-legged on the pile of matts which had been Ferwar's. With a wave of beringed hand the girl indicated the smaller collection of woven rush squares which were of her own making and had been her bed-place.

He seated himself limberly in the same fashion. It was odd what she was finding out about this stranger. His smile was gone from his lips but it still seemed to hold in his eyes which had opened to their widest extent when he looked at her and now remained that way.

"Those who are kin say 'Chan', my friends 'Yun'."

She gave another combing toss to her hair. To sit here in idle talk was not enough. There was that she must know and as soon as she might.

"Tell me now," she commanded, "what dealing have you with Lord Arfellen that his guards follow you and yet you would have none of them? Do you know that he has only to crook his finger joint so much as this," she stretched out her ringed thumb and made a slight curve in the air, "and he can have the life of near any one in Kuxortal, and set to tremble a few more he could not kill at once? What have you done?"

This Thom did not seem in the least disturbed by her questions now. He sat as easily as if he were any Burrower. In fact easier than any who would now dare to enter *this* particular chamber.

"I asked questions—questions concerning my brother who went off into your world some seasons ago and of whom there had been no word since, though he was pledged to a meeting he would not have missed unless he had met with dire trouble. You spoke of him as a witling who went into the Hard Hills. I swear to you that no matter how it would seem to your people he had good reason to go there, to hunt what he had come to discover. Now—" he hesitated for a moment and then added with the sharpness of a Guild man voicing an order, "can you tell me any other rumors concerning him? Or why anyone would wish him to come to ill?"

"There were tens of tens ways in which he could have come to ill," she returned, striving to keep her voice as cool and stern as his own. "The Hard Hills have their secrets in plenty. Most men travel by river or by sea. It used to be long ago—when I was very young, that caravans still came in from Qurux across the desert lands which front the Hard Hills. Those were from Semmele and they brought strange things from the north for the trading. Then - we heard of a plague which made Semmele a place of dead men and ghosts, and no caravans came. What they had ever brought was little—the Guilds could well make up the yield from the river men. So the way there was lost. Yes, there was talk when the off-worlder hunted out three of the old caravan men. They say he offered a fortune in broke-bits for a guide. Two of them would have none of his urging—the other got into a shuffle with one of Lord Arfellen's guards and thereafter agreed to go." She was suddenly aware of what she had said and repeated slowly, "Lord Arfellen's guard . . ." more to herself than to him.

"So and so." He used the trader's speech so easily that if she shut her eyes she could not be sure he was not of Kuxortal. "These other two—are they still here?"

The girl shrugged. "If they are, surely Gathar will find them for you. Have you not already made such a bargain with him?"

Again he was smiling. "Your knowledge seems to stretch a long way, Gentlefem Simsa. Does it touch any more on such as this?" He patted with his hand the belt pouch into which he had put the carvings.

"All I know is that the Old One had a liking for such. What I found, what was brought to her, she kept."

"What you found—where?" He caught that up eagerly.

"In the Burrows. We dig into the back years of Kuxortal, we who live on her refuse. Some of that refuse being very old. Once this," again she gestured, "might well have been part of some Lord's palace place. There are bits of of wall paint still in yonder corner. Things have been lost as houses collapsed, were built over. Kuxortal was sacked by pirates, three times attacked by armies before the rise of the River lords and their alliance. There has been much destroyed and built upon over and over again. The Burrowers live in the past, and on what they can scoop from their tunnels. We are less than dust to the Guild Lords."

"Even in your place here you must have heard things from the upper city," he seemed unable to take his eyes from her silver hair, he studied her, Simsa began to think, as if *she* were some bit or piece turned up in the underways, "what do you know of Lord Arfellen?"

Her interest was caught now. He was speaking to her as an equal, something which had never happened as far as she could remember. To the Old One she had always been a child, to the Burrowers a stranger, though she had been born among them she was sure. Yet none of them had ever matched her coloring of skin or hair. To Gathar, her main contact in the upper city, she was only a young one of a people his kind had long held in contempt. Though her management of the zorsals had won grudging respect in so far as it aided him. But to this off-worlder she was a person one asked advice of, one whose knowledge and opinions were held in the same esteem as if he were speaking to one of the upper town.

"He is the richest of the Guild Lords, his line the oldest," she began. "It is he who is the first signer every third season on the trade wares brought in. He is not seen often—having many to be hands and feet for him. He is—" she moistened her lips with tongue tip—what she would say now as pure conjecture and rumor and she hesitated to add that to pad out the little she did know.

"There is something else," he broke that minute of silence.

"They tell tales about him, that he is hunted in one place and cannot be found, later he comes from there and says that he was always there. He is said to go to none of the temples on the heights as do the other lords, but he keeps in his service one who talks with the dead. And that he is a seeker—"

"A seeker!" Thom pounced upon that as Zass would upon a ver-rat. "Is it also rumored as to what he seeks?"

"Treasure. Yet that he does not need, for much flows ever into his stronghold and little comes out again. He hires many guards and sometimes those travel up river. Their leader may come back next season but they do not. Perhaps he sells them as fighters to the River Lords—there is always quarreling there still."

"You have never heard of him sending to the Hard Hills?"

Simsa laughed. "All the treasure in the world would not send him there. No one goes in that direction, I tell you, no one."

"But one shall," he leaned a little forward, caught her gaze with his and held it steady. "For I shall, Gentlefem."

"Then you will die—as did your brother." She refused to be impressed by more than his folly.

"I think not." Now he took from his pouch the two bits of carving he had bought from her. "This I have to tell you, Gentlefem—but first answer me—how safe are you in these Burrows of yours?"

"Safe? Why do you ask that?"

Before he could answer, Zass straightened up on her perch over the low door of the Burrow. She flung back her head and gave a cry which brought Simsa upstanding, her claws expanding instantly in answer to an alarm which had reached her brain less than a second earlier. Then through the door itself came two winged creatures. As each seemed to erupt into the chamber, so swift was its emergence from the tunnel beyond, it gave a deeper cry in answer to Zass's welcome, before both planed down to stand before the girl.

There was no mistaking these—Zass's sons. That they were here meant some catastrophe at their abiding place—the warehouse. The alien caught at her hand.

"Can they be followed?"

"Not save by another of their kind. And there are none such I know of who are so trained. But—" She looked from the zorsals to the off-worlder. "I do not understand what they are doing here. They would not have left Gathar for any reason unless—unless there is trouble there! Was that the reason you asked of me concerning safety? What has happened to Gathar?" More important what might happen to her who was well known to have dealings with that waremaster even if it were only because of the zorsals? Plenty knew that she had trained them and only rented out the creature's services, refusing to sell them to him.

"I did not get your silver from him," the off-worlder returned. "When I would have gone back to his place I saw the badges of Arfellen on men at his door. And I had already had warning that my questions had startled the lord. I do not know what he seeks—I have no reason to be connected with any trade trouble which he may have. But one of the star crew passed me a message that much concerning me has been asked of the captain and that he has received orders that when the ship lifts I am not to remain."

"Yet you came to me!" She spat that in pure anger and wanted nothing more so much as to claw mark that smooth, ivory skin of his so that neither friend nor foe could put rightful name to him again. Only, one ruled by anger, as the Old One had long ago taught her, made fatal mistakes.

"Because I had to, not only to get what you showed me and what is perhaps a very important pointer to that which I seek, but because you might now be my only contact to gather the knowledge I would have. At any rate," he did not drop his gaze, there was even a shadow smile at the corner of his mouth, "is it not true that any who have had dealings with Gathar in any way can now be suspected of whatever irregularity which it will be claimed he is concerned in?"

"What do you want of me?" Both zorsals had crept very close to her feet, were looking up in her face, and uttering small cries as if they would have reassurance. Whatever had driven them from their comfortable quarters had been bad enough to bring them here in open fear.

"A hiding place, whatever knowledge you can glean,

and a way to reach the Hard Hills," he told her as if he were merely reciting items from some trader's list.

She wanted to screech at him in a voice as harsh as Zass's that she was no worker of powerful fortune. Judging by what she had heard, and now guessed from the arrival of the zorsals, they had been lucky in that they were still uncaptured. Simsa looked about the cavern a little wildly. She had always considered herself a cool and careful person, one who planned and thought before she tried any action. She was beginning to lose confidence in herself.

No. She bit her lip. There was enough installed by Ferwar's harsh training to hold her together now. She could think still, plan— For a start she looked to the zorsals and uttered the single short cry which was her order to search. Zass had not descended from her door perch, now she, too, urged her offspring to their duty, sending them out again to hide and spy along the Burrows.

From any of the kind who dwelt here they would have no help at all. Ferwar had been feared in her day, Simsa resented, and, after her besting of Baslter, hated by more than one. They would be eager to reveal to any who came seeking where exactly the prey might have taken cover. Then she and this twice damned off-worlder would be dug out as easily as one dug a well steamed or-crab out of its shell.

There was only one choice and it was being forced upon her in too swift and too sharp a way—she wanted time to plan and she knew that she had none. With this off-worlder at her heels, she could not melt away again in a shadow role. Anywhere in Kuxortal, he would be as visible as a lighted lamp in a night-dark room.

"This way."

She had wheeled about, went to pull up the sleep mats which had formed Ferwar's bed place to reveal the secret the Old One had guarded with her own body for seasons of years, judging by the work done on it, and which Simsa herself did not know in all its parts. He joined her without asking, bundling aside the mats she pushed towards him. What lay underneath in the poor light of the Burrow was a long stone seemingly as fixed as a rooted plant. However the girl, who had learned the secret once when she had tripped over Zass and had fallen with hands outstretched, now knelt and set the palms of her hands hard in certain very shallow indentations she could feel but not see.

The end of the stone rose as she bore down with her full strength. A musty odor puffed into their faces. Simsa clucked to Zass—knowing she need not recall the other two, for they could trace their dam to the end of this way with ease. She picked up the lamp in one hand, bundled the zorsal up against her with the other, and descended the shallow steps waiting there. The off-worlder swung down behind her. She did not turn her head as she said:

"There is a hold on the stone, fit your hand to it, close this way after us." She descended as rapidly as she could to give him the room he need to obey her orders. Then she stood in a very narrow runway which was thick dust underfoot but which had air with a distinct smell of the river. This was a way out she believed that even Burrowers might take a lengthy time discovering. They could reach the riverside among the refuse dumps—beyond that she would not try yet to plan.

5.

A smell of the sea tainted with the stench from the refuse dumps met Simsa as she wriggled through the last opening, Zass hopped ahead, grumbled gutturally to herself, the off-worlder kept to more laborous passage behind. Then they were out in the night — though Simsa believed that dawn could not be far distant. She sidled forward with no hope of avoiding all the pitfalls of water-washed trash, the pools of putrid matter, holding one hand across her mouth and nose to screen out what was possible, and regretting that so soon her hard-earned new clothing was thus being reduced to less than the rags she had discarded them for.

Once away from the worst of the heaps, on the part of sand the incoming tide washed clear by dripping rush, she turned quickly to her companion.

"Your ship lies there—" she kept her voice low. However, she had caught his arm in the dark, dragged him about to face the distant glow of light marking the landing field. "You can reach it from seaward."

"I have no ship to reach," he returned.

"You are off-world—" Simsa had yet to understand just what part the Guild Lords could play in the future of any starman. Certainly they could not touch nor hold him.

83

They cared too much for the star trade to anger the off-worlders who manned those ships by making any move against a member of their company. All in Kuxortal knew only too well what might follow any interference with the ship people.

"I am on my own here," he answered.

"You said that Lord Arfellen has given word that when the ship lifts you are not to remain—" she pointed out hotly.

"I have certain duties which no ship's captain can question. I came here to hunt for a man. Nor shall I leave until I find him, or else have certain knowledge of what has happened to him—more than a general word that he has vanished in a territory which no one seems to know anything about and that no search has made for him thereafter."

"And how do you get to the Hard Hills then to do that hunting?" Simsa wanted to know. "You will not gain any aid from the men of Kuxortal, not if Lord Arfellen has declared it to be thus."

She could not see him clearly, he was only a darker blot in the night. When he answered, it was calmly and with a note in his voice which made her uneasy.

"There are always ways one can get anything one truly sets all his energy and desire upon gaining. Yes, I shall see the Hard Hills. However, what happens now to you?"

"So at last your mind turns to that?" she snapped. "Kuxortal is no place for me if Gathar is in trouble. All who had dealings with him shall suffer—for the Guildmen can nose out a trail half a year cold if they wish. Also the Burrowers will not shield me. I was the Old One's eyes, feet, and ears—while she lived. Now I am fair game."

"Why did they fear her?"

Simsa did not know why she lingered here arguing with this alien. She owed him no explanations. Only—where might she go now? Gathar who had been her one contact with the upper town, could no longer be depended upon. She had a bag heavy with broken bits weighing down one sleeve. But bought men and women stayed bought only so long as they were not offered more—either in silver or in freedom from danger—by another.

"They thought she had a seeing eye. That was not true. She only knew a great deal about people—she could look into their faces, listen to their voices when her eyesight dimmed the more, and tell much of what they fought or felt. She could read and she could speak with many strangers in their own language. She was—different—not a true Burrower. I do not know her beginnings but they must have lain far from where she landed. Now—why do we waste time speaking of a dead woman? You had best go to your ship—if you would stay alive—"

"And you?" her persisted.

Did he believe he owed her something? He did not, unless she demanded it. Any more than she was responsible for him, though she had been forced to aid him after a fashion this night.

"I will go my own way—"

"Where?"

She felt as if he had her pinned helplessly against a Burrow wall, held so by his questioning alone. It was not his affair that she might find Kuxortal now too dangerous. But where *would* she go? For a moment the chill of panic shook her before she forced it under control.

From overhead came a chittering. Her head moved a

little as she answered that with a click of tongue, even as Zass, squatting near unseen at her feet, also voiced a cry. The two younger zorsals she had loosed in the Burrows had found them. So—with them to protect and be her eyes and ears—she had a better chance.

"If we head north," the off-worlder continued, "going along the shore, to where will we come?"

"We—?" she questioned. "You think that I shall go with you?"

"Have you a better plan?" he countered.

She wanted so much to say "yes," still knew that she could not. His question had shaken her thoughts out of the whirl of uncertainty to a point where she was trying to see ahead a little.

"If one follows the shoreline"—she would not say "we"—"there is a little fishing village some distance on. This part of the shore is not good—there is so much refuse spewed into the waters. Also the best anchorage below the city is for Guild-tied ships and they will not permit that to be used even in the times when no fleet comes in. Beyond the fishers there is only barren land to rim the desert. That is the Coast of Dead Men, where there is no water to be found—only sand and rock, and things which can live on both and do."

"For how long does this coast of Dead Men continue?"

Simsa shrugged, though she knew he could not see such a gesture. "Forever, perhaps. No man has ever in my hearing spoken of an end. There are long reefs out to sea which can claw open the hull of a boat as easily as Zass can crack a ver-rat bone between her teeth. Men do not bear north, unless the sea itself turns against them with some storm. Those who do are never seen again."

"However, if one goes far enough along the coast one

can come northward to the same general latitude as the Hard Hills. Yes, it might be done!" he suggested.

"By spirits who have conveniently left their bodies behind them!" Simsa retorted.

"North, you say—" He was moving away. Not even waiting to see if she was coming, too. Simsa seethed. He had pulled her into this black trouble, and now she must agree to this new utter folly he suggested, at least a portion of it, or be left to confront too many enemies on too many levels of the city which had always been her home and given her what small security she had known.

She spat out several burning and bitter words, the vilest in her vocabulary, stooped and picked up Zass, to set her on the usual shoulder perch, and then went after him, the two other zorsals taking once more to the air. At least with them for scouts she need not fear a surprise attack.

Nor did the off-worlder wait for her to catch up. He took her so much for granted did he, that he was sure she would follow? The girl would have given anything to be able to take off in the opposite direction. She debated, as she went, whether she could just have made some kind of a case for herself by heading back to the star port and betraying him to his fellows. At least her chances of not being drawn in herself would be better with the star crew then with any of the Lord Arfellen's men. *That* was wisdom as she had learned it in her Burrower years. Why then was she prowling along behind this stranger, half committed to his plans? Because she had no real answer to that question, Simsa was angry with herself, ready to lash out at the first chance she was given to unload this tangle of emotions she could not form into decent and regular order.

They were beyond the refuse heaps now and she

breathed heavily of the cleaner sea air. The starman, she noted, in the slowly graying light rising over the sea itself was hurrying. Also he was walking with long strides where the waves washed to erase his tracks. Simsa halted for a moment, pulled off her sandals, and followed his lead again, feeling the rise of the water about her bare feet and ankles, soaking the ends of her tight trousers where they were bound about her shins.

The fishing village showed lights ahead. Simsa, with extra long strides, caught up with her companion, pulling his arm.

"Their boats go out before dawn," she told him. "The haverings run then. If you do not want half the world to know what you desire to do, for the present you will wait."

He slowed for a step or so and looked down at her. In this very faint light she could see his face only as a light blur, she thought perhaps he might not be able to see her at all. Until she remembered her hair, and dropped her hold on him to hastily draw out a length of head cloth, binding that into a secure head covering.

"Wait for what?" he asked. "If we want to have a boat—"

"You will not deal with the Headman," she retorted, knotting her scarf with a last twist, made so viciously tight because of her perturbation that she could have cried out in pain. "Let the men go. It is with the House mistress of the Headman that any bargain should be made. Lustita—if she is still ruling in that house—will always have the final word."

"You know her?"

"A little. She had some dealings with the Old One once or twice. She is a woman who likes a heavy purse in her sleeve, and not having it known to her man that she carries such. You wait here. I shall see—" She had taken a step or two past him and then she looked back curiously.

"How do you know that I am not going to cry up those who will hold you for Lord Arfellen?" she asked.

"That you ask me that— No, I do not fear betrayal, Lady Simsa. You have had good chances in plenty to do that several times this night and have not taken them."

"You trust too easily and too much!" The wrath she had been holding so long broke then. She could have screamed at him. "Had I been taken with you what story could I have told which would have saved me? Me, the lowest of what Lord Arfellen would deem harbor scum? You must not trust me—nor anyone."

"Wait—" He had unsealed the front of his tightly fitting uniform. Now he tossed her a small bag which she caught without thinking. "If your Headman's woman wants pay—give it to her. Ask in return a boat—a small one which I must see before the bargain is complete—also provisions. Sweeten her with part of this and promise her more only when all is ready."

The bag was heavy—though so small. No bits of silver in that, Simsa was sure. She said nothing but went, grim-faced as she padded along on the sand. So he thought so little of her warning that he put this in her hands? She hated him hotly for slighting her so, making it now impossible for her to do anything but her best to carry out his insane plan. She would get him his boat—if she possibly could—and what he wanted in it—but that would be the end. This village was as far away as they would continue to travel together.

The sun was well up, lighting a narrow tongue of the

sea which formed a cove hardly large enough to run the small craft into shoreward. Simsa sat on her heels well shadowed by rocks, Zass on a tall, weed draped stone near her, dividing her attention between the labors of the offworlder and the cliff above, where their two other zorsals taking up sentry posts, intent, the girl trusted, on both land and sea approaches to this hideout.

She was sure after the first few moments of her trafficking with Lustita that this had not been the first such transaction which the House mistress had conducted. She had looked at the trade bar stamped with the seal of the Metal Guild, weighed it in one large red hand, then had demanded:

"For what?" Bluntly, as if Simsa merely was bargaining for a catch of spaeels.

"For a boat, foremost, a seaworthy one," the girl had answered as tersely, "later—he who sent this will ask for the rest."

The woman's small eyes had narrowed until they seemed no larger than the pits of varc fruit buried in an oversized brown pudding. Then she had nodded.

"Well enough. Go to where there are two standing rocks on the cliff. Those look like fingers raised in a scorn sign. Wait there—"

She had scooped the single bar up with a hand large enough to hold the whole of it. Though Simsa was certain that she herself had been recognized as the fetch-and-carry for the Old One, nothing in Lustita's eyes, voice, or expression revealed that. She felt a little easier in her mind, certain that she had read this woman aright.

They had gone inland, twice creeping flat on their bellies to round ends of cultivated garden fields, but had reached the appointed rendezvous well before the sun was high. Nor had they been there long before Lustita, walking easily in spite of a huge basket making a shoulder burden which could weigh as much as a small man, rounded the point of that narrow inlet. She had a rake in one hand, was methodically harvesting streamers of the dark red weed, which, when dried, could be ground into powder and sold for fertilizer on those same fields past which they had earlier crawled.

Simsa arose from behind the rocks just long enough for the fisherwoman to sight her, then ducked down again. Without missing a single strand of the weed, Lustita reached them, though Simsa had to call on patience to wait out her arrival.

Lustita gave a grunt, resting her leaking basket on a rock top, leaning back against the same support. The off-worlder stood face to face her, but did not come completely out of hiding. There was no change on the woman's stolid face.

"A boat—she said—" Lustita gave the slightest of nods towards Simsa. "What else then?"

"What all is needful to get that same boat along the coast." He spoke the straight trade language with its different inflections of speech, but Lustita had enough dealings in Kuxortal to understand. "Provisions, water—charts of the shoreline—"

Her scanty eyebrows slid up. "Why not bargain for a High Lord's own shallop?" she returned. "Boat, yes, that can be done. Frankis has been drunk once too often, his house mistress would be glad to earn a bit, and also teach him a lesson. He lies now in the watch house where he tends a smarting back for having landed too good a blow on a Guild guard, so he shall not be free for ten tens of days—maybe still longer. Provisions—yes, those can be gathered, a few here, a few there. And there will be no questions if they are brought together so. Charts—" she grinned showing gaps between big yellowed teeth, "we have none such. Our men carry their sea-lore in their heads—and beat it into their sons when the time comes. A sore back makes a lad remember very well. If you would take to the sea it will be by your own fortune and none borrowed from us."

"Very well." Simsa suspected that the off-worlder had really not expected much different an answer.

"I have one bar of trade metal," Lustita continued. "Shall we say five more?"

"Shall we say a thousand?" Simsa countered. Caution made her object. Pay the first toll mentioned, and they would arouse the woman's interest in them to the point where she might consider she could perhaps deal even more profitably with others. There was only the situation of their village which linked the river traders with the sea farers, the fisherfolk were not too much in awe of the guilds. Even the laws of Kuxortal did not touch them, save when, as the unlucky Frankis, they fell into trouble within the city itself.

Lustita shrugged and her basket wavered a little. "Those who would purchase help cannot keep fast hand on the purse," she commented. "Well enough—make it four then. But less than that I shall not go. It will take time—though the boat will come first."

"How much time?" the starman wanted to know.

"A day—maybe part of the night. Things done in caution cannot be hurried. You shall have full measure. Give me half more now—"

Reluctantly Simsa obeyed the nod of the alien and slid two more of the bars from the purse which she kept carefully concealed within her sleeve. Lustita must not be able to see the size or weight of that.

Though she had expressed not the slightest surprise upon discovering that one of those with whom she must bargain was an off-worlder, her outward indifference could mean little. Simsa did not trust her, though she believed from what she knew of the fisherwoman's dealings with the Old One that the woman was close mouthed in her own way. And she owed no service to the guild men.

The boat had arrived even as she promised, propelled by two bare-legged, bare-armed, girls, who also had weed baskets with them. They had tied up the craft, scrambled out, shouldered their baskets and went on their way, carefully never raising their eyes from what they did, splashing off as if well pleased to be done with a bothersome task.

Simsa continued to sit behind her rock, watching the off-worlder carefully inspect the craft. It was not made for far sailing, though it had a single mast. She guessed it used mainly for coast traveling when the spaeels came inshore to lay their eggs, and that it would not last long in storm-tossed open water. But the way the starman went about his examination impressed her in spite of herself. It was evident that he was familiar with boats not unlike this one, no matter on what strange other world he had gained such knowledge. When he at last came back to her hidden cranny he flung himself down with a sigh as if some small part of a heavy burden had slipped from him.

"It is a stout craft," he commented, "with a shallow draw—such as can well go exploring along the coast—"

"A coast with teeth such as you have never seen—hard rock teeth!" she retorted. "And what if you do spy your

Hard Hills inland? They will be well back from the coast — you will have no way of reaching them. You could not carry food and water to make such a trip, and, even if you reached the Hills, you would only die there."

"Lady Simsa," he rolled over on his back, flinging one arm up to half shadow his face and screen his eyes from the sun, which had found its way into their cranny, "what legends do they tell of this Hard Hills country?"

She cupped up a handful of sand, allowed the fine grit to shift away through loose-locked fingers. "What they always say of the unknown — that there is death waiting there. Oh, they talk of treasure waiting too, but no man is mad enough to go hunting it. That is no bargain to be sought."

"Yet I have seen things which came out of those Hills — strange and wondrous things — "

Simsa stared at him. "Where? Not in Kuxortal!" She could be emphatic about that. Such tales would have filtered down the city long since — even to the Burrows.

"I have seen such on another world," he told her. "When the star ships found this world there was no landing field at Kuxortal. Ships came and went before the Guilds even knew that they had planeted here."

Which could be true, she decided, for the land was large and they had certain knowledge only of those parts the traders traveled.

"One such ship landed in the midst of what you call the Hard Hills. The cargo it brought back was such that the least man aboard her was wealthy beyond dreams — "

The girl was very still. Wealth beyond the dreams of the star men! What could that buy one — even one out of the Burrows with no name, no kin, perhaps the Guilds sniffing at her heels?

"Your brother sought that?" No wonder Lord Arfellen was alerted if this story was true. No Guild Lord ever had enough in the way of treasure to be beyond *his* dreams!

"Yes—not the treasure for itself though—but for the knowledge which lay with it. The ship which returned had certain other finds."

"If a ship could land there once—why not again?" she demanded with instant suspicion.

"Their landing was a forced one. In getting free there was great difficulty—they were very lucky—it would not be tried a second time. But I have all the information my brother had, I know near where to look. I am not quite the fool you have been thinking me—Lady Simsa."

"You still have to cross the desert and you cannot carry enough supplies. Your brother went with one of the wandering folk and only one of those would go—he never came back."

"All true." He nodded, the sand catching in his black hair as his head moved. "However, it is not in my family to leave one of their own lost. There will be ways to fight even the desert, my lady—"

"Why do you call me that?" she suddenly demanded. "I am no kin to any of the High Lords. I am Simsa—"

"But not a Burrower, I think," he answered her.

She scowled at the rock. Before she could make answer to that there was more splashing in the water. They huddled down behind the rock watching though the zorsals had given no warning.

The same girls who had brought the boat were coming back. Their basket thongs cut deeply into their thin shoulders near bowing them over like old women. Again, paying no attention to the upper part of the cove or the rocks behind which the two hid, they proceeded to down those baskets, scoop out armloads of weed and then dump unto the sand closely woven hampers which they left lying, as they reloaded their much lightened burdens to make off again.

There were other visitors during the afternoon, each bringing baskets, some large, some small. The last came after twilight. Lustita herself in an oared boat containing six jars near as tall as Simsa herself, but empty. These the fisherwoman told them could be filled with water at a spring a short distance to the north. She accepted the last two bars, but before she left she offered a half warning:

"There is trouble in the city—the guards have been out." She spat noisily into the heavy wash of wave. "They have not yet come beyond the north gate. But there has not been such a boiling up since the underwater spirits set the big run of the gar when I was a little maid."

Thom looked to the girl as the woman tramped away. "I take it that we have been missed—"

"*You* have been missed!" she corrected him sharply.

"I think—"

But what he thought was never to be uttered then for both zorsals on the cliffs above took wing and came fluttering and wheeling down. Simsa did not need their hooting cries, through the deepening dusk, to know that they had sighted more than just the usual coming and going along the coast. The starman seized her hand. She had only time to catch up Zass before he pulled her towards the boat, half threw her on board, told her harshly to stay where she was.

He had brought out a long pole and braced it against the rocks. His shoulders tensed in what she could see was a great effort, he pushed them out, away from the narrow cove. They were in the open sea beyond when she caught a wink of lights on the cliff top, saw one of those on its way down, and understood that the chase had not been dropped, that somehow they had been traced.

Simsa did not like the sea. She found the pitching and rolling of the small boat terrifying, though she would not have allowed her companion to guess at her fear. Nor did she linger when they tied up again, but unbidden helped him to fill the water jars, transport them down and stow them with special care. He had already, during the day, stowed to the best advantage the rest of their small cargo of supplies, and at the time had called her attention to the fact that Lustita had included both fishing lines and a small net in their equipment.

The zorsals settled together on the edge of the small casing over the middle part of the deck which was the only protection against wind and spray. While the offworlder stepped the small mast, set a triangle of sail to catch the night wind. He took the tiller, and swung the craft north while Simsa crouched under the shelter and wished herself back in the Burrows, ragged, hungry, but with safe and solid land under her two feet.

She had never meant to come this far. It had been her firm intention to bid the alien good fortune and hide out perhaps in the fishing village, even if it cost her most of her gains. But events had all come so suddenly, she was left with no choice—not for now.

However, she decided firmly, as the boat scudded along its way and queasiness made her hate her body, she would never go into the desert! Let this witling of an offworlder take sight of his hills and tramp off to bake to death among them, she would stay with the boat when that hour came and somehow find a way back. She began to enlarge upon that plan. One could claim to be the survivor of a ship wreck, she thought, even if she knew so little of the sea that she might not deceive any true sailor. Yes, that was it—a traveler from over-seas—wrecked—

She would have plenty of time, maybe days of it, to plan her story. And, being Simsa, she would think up a very good one. After all it was only zorsals that could make her true identity known. Those should be happy enough to return to a free life in the wilds, leaving her to play the role she decided upon. Settling her crossed arms upon her drawn up knees the girl rested her chin upon them and busied herself with plans, so hoping to forget the unpleasant churning in her middle.

6.

The sun threw a burning blight over the land. Simsa had covered as much of her skin against those rays as she could, smearing on fat she had skimmed from one of the jars of fresal soup they had eaten early during the voyage. As she drew herself up to stand beside the off-worlder on a baked rock which radiated heat as might a cook hole, she knew how impossible were the plans this Thom had made and added to all during that nightmare of a sea journey. Let him go out into that white hot furnace and frizzle into cinders, she would take her chance with the sea again, as horrible as that had been. Even at the thought of what she had endured the past two days while they had been tossed about by what her companion had persisted in calling a "fresh wind" made her nurse her empty and sore stomach with hands that were cracked and bleeding from the salt water and rope burns—for, as untrained as she was, she had had to lend her strength to their battle against the power of wind and wave.

Before them stretched such a forsaken land as might have been painted as a lesson to discourage any traveler. There were drifts of sand, their white surface spread under this sun to sear the eyes. When there was no sand, rock, worn and scraped by wind-driven grit for more

101

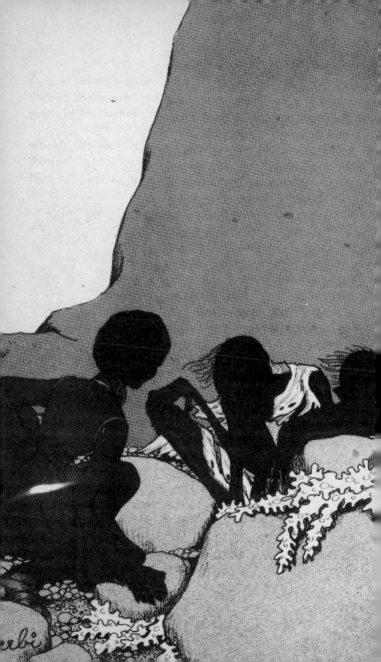

seasons than a man could count, made reefs on land as toothed and forbidding as those reefs through which they had somehow found a way at sea. There was nothing which could live there—

Only, the off-worlder was not surveying the deadly land which stretched forth from the very foot of the cliff up which they had found their way. Instead he had slipped from one of the loops upon his belt a set of distance glasses which had been folded into themselves, opened them and tinkered with their setting. Now, by their aid, he surveyed the country beyond where heat haze shimmered. Here and there in the middle distance a spume of sand arose, as if by the bidding of an unseen enemy, to whirl and dance. By squinting between the fingers with which she had quickly shaded her eyes, Simsa could just make out a vague line across the far horizon. The Hard Hills perhaps. Not that she cared.

She turned her back determinedly upon the whole threat of the land and had begun to edge toward the descent from that lookout, when an exclamation from her companion stopped her. When she glanced up she saw that he now pointed those distance glasses not toward the distant goal but rather downward toward the desert land itself.

"That is the way—"

"What way?" Even two words seemed to crack her lips.

"Our road!" He folded the glasses back, was fitting them into their loop. Simsa was too worn to argue with a madman. If he thought he had found some road, let him take it and be gone. She had been caught too long in the trap of his plans and must free herself before she lost what energy she had left.

Now she asked no questions, merely swung over and

began the crawl down the cliff side to the bay where their boat, bearing the signs of its rough passage, rocked in what small waves found their way past the reefs to this pocket which was nearly as narrow and hidden as the one that Lustita had chosen for the outset of this miserable voyage.

As the girl neared the narrow strip of hard pebbles (there was no sand on this side of the cliff) which lined the shore, she averted her eyes from what had greeted her when she made the first awkward leap from boat to shingle. There lay evidence of what this dread coast could do. Still, the off-worlder had not shown the slightest dismay when he had viewed it.

Two withered, shrunken bodies, or the remains of such, had been somehow wedged between the rocks. Or had they crawled there during their last spurt of life energy to find their own tombs? A few faded, colorless rags still clung to the blackened, shrunken flesh. Simsa was glad that the heads had fallen forward so that she need not look upon what long-ago death had made of their faces; there were no birds here, no crabs or other sea spawned vermin, to clean their bones. Rather they had simply blackened under that sun to fearsome representations of what seemed to be more demons than once-living men.

Now Thom again passed them without a glance, striding along the sliding pebbles which were quick to shift under his boots so that he balanced as he went, heading farther north. When he scrambled over the rocks guarding the other end of this small bay she pulled herself to her feet to follow. Somehow she could not remain where she was — along with those blackened things which she was ever aware were at her back, whether she looked in their direction or not.

Her feet slipped and slid so in the sandals that she had made patches of covering for both sandal and skin from parts of a rent sail she had found stored on the boat, twisting the thick stuff and knotting it as tightly as she could. Also she picked her way with care, having no desire to fall. She was a fool—it would be better to crawl back under the closed part of the ship where the zorsals whimpered now and then. Though she had emptied a hamper and made them a kind of nest away from the sun, she could do nothing more to spare them the heat.

This scramble over the rocks brought her a fall which scraped a good strip of skin from the side of one hand. She could no longer suppress her misery as she had sworn to do. Forcing herself to the edge of the water to dip her hand in the harsh smart of the sea, she whimpered like the zorsals, allowing herself that small outlet for her emotions. The off-worlder was far enough ahead now that he certainly could not hear her for she had determined from the first that he would have no complaint from her.

There was another indentation of the coast beyond the rocks where she had slipped, a much wider beach in the shape of a triangle, its point running landwards between the walls of the cliff. Thom was just disappearing into that point, and, even as she squatted, nursing her smarting hand against her breast, he disappeared entirely. There must be some break or cave—

The thought of a cave and what it might mean as a refuge from the sun drew her on with a return of strength she could not have believed earlier she could summon. Thus she stumbled and wavered across the sand where Thom's prints were formless depressions.

Only this was not the cave she had longed for—rather a cleft leading inwards, a break in the desert floor which might, in some very long time ago, have furnished a bed for a river. If this thrice cursed land had ever held any water at all.

There was the same sand and gravel for footing, but the rock walls on either side where sheer here, offering no holds, Simsa thought, that one might use to reach the surface of the land above. While out of the cut came a breath of fire worse than any the sun had dealt already, as if the cleft was a furnace meant to draw the worst of the heat and hold it.

Even Thom must have found it too much, for he was returning, having gone only a short distance inland. To her surprise he was smiling, and there was a spring in his step as if he had come upon a well all ringed about with greenery, water gushing forth to run headlong. Simsa wondered for a moment or two if the off-worlder had indeed been driven mad by the heat and the barrenness of this part of the world. She had heard tales of the desert madness and how travelers were led astray there by images of that which had never existed.

"We have our road!" he told her.

"There?" He was mad. She edged away from him crab fashion, refusing to take her eyes from him lest his insanity take a murderous turn and he savage her.

"There!" he agreed, to her continued horror. Then he must have read the thought behind her expression for he added quickly:

"Not by day, no. But at night—then it will be different. I did not come here without knowledge of such travel. There is coolness at night in such a land as this. The sea wind carries moisture with it and that condenses against the rocks. We can go this way—taking water and food with us—you shall see. I have done this on other worlds."

Simsa shut her mouth. There was no use in raising any argument. If he said they could sprout wings and fly inland, then she must agree with him for this moment. He believed he spoke the truth and she wanted no part of any struggle with him. It was enough for now that he was willing to return to the boat, come into the poor shade they could find there, though he did not stretch out to lie panting, only half conscious, as she was forced to do; her efforts had brought an end to even that wiry strength she had developed over the years of her Burrow life.

During the latter part of the day she either slept or else lost consciousness, she was never sure just which. Only that, for a while, she had watched him ripping loose part of the ship's planking, and, using ropes he wet in the sea and then knotted about these boards, pushing that knotted portion out into the sun to dry hard and stiff.

Once or twice she wavered into enough wakefulness to want to protest his so battering a ship she fully intended to use for her own escape. Only, before she could summon either the strenth or the words to do so, she lapsed once more into that daze of misery.

There came an end to the day at last. The sun crawled down the cloudless sky, and a broad banner of color touched the waves far out, sending a last glare into her smarting eyes as she drew herself over to give water to the zorsals whose plaintive cries had become so faint a croaking that alarm had shaken her into action.

They lay in a forlorn heap, their mouths open, their antennae limp, their eyes closed, while breaths which were gasps for life itself lifted their furred breasts. Simsa paid no attention to the off-worlder who had now gone ashore to work at whatever had kept him busy. She forced the tight capping from one of the water jars (one of the last two which were entirely full) and held a pannikan with shaking hands as she dribbled into it the precious liquid, near counting the drops. Her body ached for a drink—she wanted to lie and just let some coolness wash over her whole sun cracked skin—.

With the pannikan in hand she crawled to the hamper nest. Zass first. The girl cradled the zorsal between her arm and her breast. With all the care she could use to keep the contents from spilling, she held the pannikan above the creature's gaping mouth, letting the moisture, which was sickly warm yet still life-giving, drip down. She could not be sure, but that body felt too hot to her, as if not only the punishing sun, but an inner fever ate at it now. At first a bit of the liquid ran from the side of the beak-like muzzle. Then she saw Zass make a convulsive effort and swallow.

Only a little—but enough that the zorsal found voice to complain plaintively when Simsa replaced her and picked up one of the others to do likewise. Carefully she shared the contents of the pannikan among them as equally as she could. The younger birds revived sooner, pulled themselves up with their clawed paws to the edge of the hamper and teetered back and forth there, one gathering enough voice to honk the cry with which they greeted dusk and hunting time.

The girl then took back Zass into her hold, supporting the Zorsal's head with her scraped hand. The creature's huge eyes were now open, and, Simsa believed, knowing. Her plan for loosing them—that she could never do here. They could not survive in a country so utterly barren and heat-blasted.

No, she must take them with her when she went—went? For the first time Simsa looked about with more understanding. What she saw now brought such a rush of fear that, in spite of the baking her body had taken most of the day, set her shivering.

The mad off-worlder! While she had been lazing away the day he had done this!

Not only had he stripped away most of the decking on the main portion of the boat, but he had taken the sail, slit it into strips. To make what? The thing which rested on the shingle was a monstrous mixture of hide-cloth from the sail, pieces of wood ripped and then retied into what looked like a small boat—except that it was flat of bottom. To it, while she had been unconscious, he had also transferred and lashed into place the rest of their food hampers, and now he was coming for the water jars. Simsa's cracked lips were splitting sore as she snarled up at him. He had left her no way of escape now.

She could either remain where she was, to die and dry like those blackened remnants behind the rocks, or be a part of his madness. Her claws came out of their sheaths, and she growled, wanting nothing more than to make a red ruin of his smooth face, his large body. At bay, the water jars behind her, she faced him ready to fight. Better to die quickly, than be baked in this furnace of a land.

He halted. At least he feared her a little. A spark of confidence awoke in Simsa at that. He had an off-world knife at his belt—port law allowed him no other weapons here. Let him use that against her claws—against the zorsals, if the creatures were recovered enough to obey her signal. She dropped Zass to the deck and heard the guttural battle cry arising in answer to her own emotion which the creature sensed. The other two lifted their wings, sidled along their perch—ready to fly, to attack—

"It is our only chance, you know," he said evenly, as if they were discussing some market bargain.

Her fingers crooked and Zass screamed. Simsa tried to throw herself forward in one of her leaps, but her weakened body did not answer. She had to put out a hand to keep herself from slamming face down upon the deck.

"You have made it so—" She raised her head a fraction to snarl at him. "Give me clean death—you have the means—" she nodded to the knife he had made no effort to draw. "I never asked, never planned—"

He did not try to come any closer. She made a weak clucking noise and the zorsals did not take flight. Kill him, she thought miserably, and she would have nothing no hope left. Did she still hope at all? She supposed that she did. All life which had a mind to think also clung to hope, even when that seemed impossible.

Not trying yet to get to her feet, the girl drew herself away on hands and knees from the water jars and let him take them—waving him towards them when he would have come to her instead. No, she would move on her own as long as she could. When that was no longer possible—well, there must be ways of ending. She would not be beholden to this mad alien for any easement now.

She accepted the food he offered her as the last signs of the sun went, the evening banners faded from the sea. She drank—no more than her share, and some of that she gave to Zass. When he returned to the thing he had made, she loosened the front of her short coat and made a place for the zorsal. The other two had already winged their way to the waiting drag thing and were perched on the lashed hampers.

Simsa followed. There was a wind now off the sea, cool. She had never believed that she would feel cool again. The touch of it reached somehow into her, clearing her thoughts—though not smothering her inner rage—giving energy to her body.

Did the alien propose to drag that thing of his? Or would he harness the both of them to it and work her as well until they both yielded to heat and exhaustion?

If that was his plan he would discover that she was not going to beg off—she would keep with him stride by stride as long as she could—or he would drive them both to the impossible. So when she came to stand beside him she looked for the drag ropes. There was only one—a single strand which she believed could not take the weight of the thing he had built.

He asked no help of her, but faced the drag carrier front on. His hand touched his belt for a moment. Then, to her amazement, the impossible happened before her eyes. There was a trembling of the carrier. It arose from the gravel and hung in the air—actually in the air—at least the height of her own knee. Picking up the lead rope, Thom set off along the narrow beach and the thing floated after him as if it were some huge wingless zorsal, as obedient to his will as her own birds were to hers.

For a long moment she simply watched what she still could not believe. Then she took off in a hurry, lest he vanish from sight. What new wonders he might bring into their service she could not guess, but now she would willingly accept all the strange tales which were told of the starmen and what they could do. Even though they never, as far as she knew, had demonstrated any such powers on this world before.

Her anger lost in her need to know how such a thing might be, Simsa slipped and slid, forgetting her drained strength until she came even with Thom who walked steadily ahead, leading his floating platform.

"What do you do?" she got out between gasps of breath as she caught up. "What makes it hang so in the air?"

She heard him actually give a chuckle, and then the look he turned on her was alive with sly humor.

"If you told those at the port what you now see, they would send me back to my home world, sentenced to stay out of space forever," he told her, though he seemed only amused at being able to explain what must be a crime among his kind. "I have merely applied to this problem something common on other planets—ones more advanced than yours. And *that* is a deadly crime according to the laws by which we abide. There is a small mechanism I planted at the right spot back there—" he pointed with his thumb over his shoulder but did not turn his head, "which nullifies gravity to a small extent—"

"Nullifies gravity," she repeated, trying to give the strange words the same sound as he had. "I do not know—some people believe in ghosts and demons, but Ferwar said they are mainly what those who believe in them make for themselves by their own fears—that you can believe in any bad dream or thing if you turn your full mind to it. But this is no ghost nor demon."

"No. It is this." They were into the cut of the valley now. The sea wind behind them made the passage more bearable now than she could ever have believed it could be when she had seen it by day. Now as he halted for a moment, it was still not too dark for her to make out what he pointed to as he repeated, "It is this."

"This" was what appeared as a black box no bigger than could be covered by his hand were he to set that palm down over it. The thing rested directly in the middle of his drag carrier, and now she could see that the cargo on board had been carefully stacked in such a way that the load must weigh evenly along the full length, leaving open only that one spot in the exact center vacant, the place in which sat the box.

"You toss a stone into the air and it falls," he said, "it is the attraction of the earth which pulls it down. But if that attraction could be broken sufficiently—then your stone would float. On my world we wear belts with such attachments which give us individual flying power when they are mated with another force. We can move also much heavier things than this with little trouble. Unfortunately I could not smuggle through the field guards as large a nullifier as I wanted. This is limited; you see how close to the ground the weight holds it.

"There is this also—the power is limited. However, it is solar powered, and here the sun can renew it, at least for the space in which I think we shall have need of it."

Simsa could understand his words easily enough but the concept they presented was so far from anything she had known that his speech was akin to a wild travel tale, such as the river traders might use to scare off the gullible from their own private ports of trade, as was well known they were apt to do. She thought of such a thing being attached to a belt so that one could share the sky with such as the zorsal, and the uses one could put such skill to.

"The Thieves Guild," she spoke aloud her own train of thought. "What they would not give for such as that! No," a shiver which was not from the cooling of the wind shook her, "no, they would kill for that! Is it such as this that Lord Arfellen would hunt you for?"

She could not understand what such a thing would mean also to even a High Guild Lord.

"No," Thom returned. "It is just what I have said; what he wanted—what I am sure he still wants—is that which we are going to find, up ahead."

That this off-world marvel gave them a better chance was what was paramount for Simsa now. Not that their way was too easy. At places the cut through which they made their way was near barricaded by fallen rocks, so that Thom had to work his towed carrier carefully around stones which it had not power enough to lift above. Heartened by the fact that they did possess such a wonder to make easier their way Simsa now hurried to lend a hand, steadying, or pushing, or helping to swing the thing back and forth to avoid its being caught.

Thom did not push the pace. At intervals he would stop to rest, more, Simsa guessed—though she did not want to admit that even to herself—on her account than from any need of his own. In the dark the zorsals came to life, the younger two even taking wing now and then. Also it would seem that this desert place held inhabitants after all, for one of her creatures, cruising high, gave a hunter's cry and struck down to make a kill among the rocks, his brother doing the same not too long after.

Simsa called them in with a whistle. The off-worlder had snapped another stud on that belt of marvels and a beam of pale light answered, forming a ray ahead. Into that the younger of the zorsals flew after a hunting hoot, a dangling thing, which seemed mostly armored tail, in his forefeet. Simsa set Zass down on the bobbing carrier and her son offered the old zorsal the fresh caught prey which she ate eagerly with a crunching of what could be either scales or bones.

During one of their stops Thom showed the girl how the cooling of the stone condensed moisture carried by the sea wind which still was pulled up the cut as if the very force of the desert would draw it in. She laid her torn hand against that damp surface and wondered if there was not some way these precious wet drops could be made to add to their store of water. Drink they did—very sparingly from one of the jars, and ate now of dried meal and fish ground together and made into cakes. The fat which bound the other ingredients together was rancid, but fishermen lived on it at sea for weeks, and this was no country for the fastidious.

Simsa had no idea how far they had gone, though her feet felt numb—where they did not ache—while the cloth she had bound about them was torn to tatters. She had been too aware of the need for watching for any obstacle which could threaten the carrier, though perhaps the off-worlder was planning to use some other amazing thing to lighten their journey tomorrow. The girl only became aware of the paling of the night sky when he paused and said:

"We cannot risk day travel. Look there ahead—see where that slide has carried down the rocks? With this," he laid hand on the side of the carrier so it swung a little under his touch, "set across the top of those we shall have a roof to give us some protection. But we must get the water jars and the food under it before sun rises."

Simsa could help with that, using care to prop each water jar stable with small stones so there might not be any chance of a spill. Zass perched first on the lightened sled, which, when all burdens were removed, shot upward until Simsa gave a cry and Thom hauled it down, bracing it, and then taking off the box and stationing it with the same care as she had used with the water jars, not within the shadow but on a flat rock where the sun would strike it.

He then touched her shoulder, half giving her a shove towards the improvised shelter.

"I am going up—" he pointed to the cliff nearest them. "Before it gets too hot I want to try my bearings and see how near we are to the Hills."

She was willing enough to leave that scramble to him, having no wish to expend further energy. Sitting down with her back to one of the rocks which supported the carrier, she busied herself with the windings about her sore feet. How foolish she had been not to bring with her a packet of Ferwar's healing herbs, she could well do with them now. There was no grease left. However, under the strips of rags which held them on her feet, the sandals were still stout enough so that she was not walking bare of foot—not yet.

Chirping to the zorsals she summoned them in, selecting a flat stone, loosing her head cloth, and coiling it there for a nest. They settled down with drowsy little mutters, their antennae close coiled, far more themselves than they had been by the shore, though they had not yet had to last through the furnace of the day. She was hungry and thirsty, but she would neither eat nor drink until Thom returned. The energy of the starman amazed her. He had worked through the heat of the past day to make the carrier; to her knowledge he had not rested. Yet he had kept going with this easy gait all through the night, and now he had made the climb to the top of the cut.

Of what were these off-worlders made—unwearing material like their mighty star ships? She did not believe that even the desert riders of the past could have done so well as Thom had done this day, or night.

There was the sound of stones falling, then, very visible in the now growing light, he landed easily, apparently jumping from a point above, only a few feet away—to move in beside her. She reached for the water pannikan. There were smears of dust across his face, and already those were muddied by sweat which trickled down his cheeks.

He drank slowly, though she was well certain that he would have gulped it in an instant had he not been prudent. She waited until he had swallowed the last drop before she asked:

"How far?"

"I am not sure—" At least he was not lying to her, and Simsa felt pride that he would not. "It is difficult to judge distances. I would say another night's travel and we would be close—if not there."

He ate doggedly the half cake she offered him, and then, without a word, curled his tall body into a position which did not overcrowd her yet still brought him full under the carrier roof, and immediately went to sleep as if that too he could do by his will alone.

7.

Simsa lay gasping in the pocket of heat. Sun shining into the crevice had turned their refuge into a pot placed over the fire. She had opened her coat, pulled loose chemise and wrappings which had stiffened with the stale sweat of her body. It was too hot to move, to think. The girl wavered in a nightmare land of half consciousness, arousing twice to tend the zorsals when she thought she could hear their gasping. If any wind blew the sand above the lip of the cut in which they rested, or sent whirling pillars of grit dancing there, it did not spill down to where they lay imprisoned.

From under swollen eyelids she glanced at the off-worlder. The upper part of his tight-fitting suit was open, he must have pulled that so without her being aware of any movement. He had turned on his back, and she saw the rise and fall of his pale-skinned chest. Yet he seemed to be asleep, as if his efforts had thrown him so far into weariness that not even the heat could awaken him.

Time dragged on so slowly the girl felt that she had lain there forever and that there would be no end to this misery. She denied herself water—keeping what she tipped so slowly from the jar they had broached the night before to succor the zorsals.

119

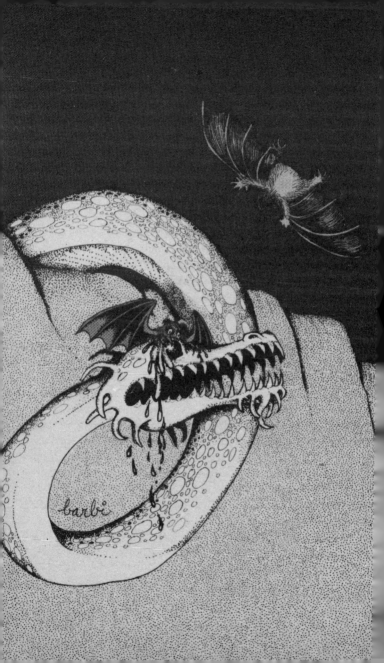

She must have slept, for there were blurred dreams which filled much of the day. She was sure that once she had lain and watched Ferwar, wrapped in the many layers of those garments which were made patch upon patch, walk down past the rock on which the off-worlder had set his magic lifting thing. A younger Ferwar that had been, her back not yet curved into a bow, not yet leaning on the staff. She had passed their refuge and gone on with the brisk step of one bound on a certain task which must be accomplished within a given time.

Simsa shaped the name of that seeming wayfarer but did not speak aloud. Only, as if she had been hailed, the tattered figure paused by the rock on which Thom had laid his treasure. From under the heavy, shaggy brows she looked straight at the girl. Then deliberately she raised the staff which she did not need now to support herself, swinging it wide so that it swept over the off-world thing. Then its tip pointed up the cut. Her lips in turn moved with words Simsa could not hear. Having surveyed their pitiful camp for a long moment, the Old One turned and went on.

It was a dream, of course, or some vision brought by the heat and the place in which she lay. Still Simsa dragged herself up well as she could and watched that walker until suddenly she was not there.

There was only one reason for her to appear now, Simsa decided, too far sunk in the misery of her body to know fear. Ferwar was dead, she would lead them on until they, too, joined her. The girl found she did not greatly care. She dropped back again, her hand curled up against her cheek. Smoothing cool touched her heated flesh, like a precious drop of water flung out of a fountain—

With the infinite slowness to which she was reduced Simsa brought up her hand and looked at the ring. Days earlier it had become too large for her shrunken flesh, but she had not put it away into safety. Instead she had wrapped the hoop around and around with torn bits of the cloth as she had used to ease her feet, wedging it so securely as she might. Now as she looked down into the cloudy, glowing gem which formed the roof of the keep it was like—almost like—gazing indeed into a pool of water.

Magic—what was magic? There was the lore of growing things to cure the body—which Ferwar had known and taught her—a little. For it had been true that the old woman had been jealous of her skill and never quick to share knowledge. There were such wonders as the off-worlder seemed to know and use. But those were only things built by men, from their own learning and efforts—solid things one could hold in one's hand.

There were the tales of strange powers. Yet no one Simsa had ever known had actually seen these in action. Always such had been viewed in another place, another time, and the girl had never accepted them as anything but tales. Knowledge could be won, then lost, and won again. Those who had lived before could be wiser than the men who came after, if something happened to interrupt the flow of their wisdom from one generation to the next.

This ring and the other pieces of jewel work she carried hidden on her were finer than any she had seen in the upper city shops when she had dared go to look upon the riches she had no hope of even laying finger on. That did not mean they were magic—merely that they were old and the fruit of labor of hands long still and dwindled into bone, even into dust.

Still as she lay there now staring down into the pool of the grey-blue gem, she was—

Walls rose about her. There was no sun, still there was heat. Fire blazed and reached out tongues to scorch her. She heard screams, wild cries, and the roar of other sounds the like of which she had never heard before. At her feet there was a pool, bordered by shimmering blocks of blue green stone. She teetered on the very rim of that, afraid to leap, afraid to stay and face a fury which raged closer and closer.

The darkness of the sky overhed was rent by great flashes of raw fire. She saw that lick at a tower and the tower swayed, came falling down. Simsa screamed and leaped into the waiting water. But it was too hot, searing her. This was death and still it would not close its jaws well upon her—rather it played with her, using torment, as a zorsal would use its claws when, filled of stomach, it played with fresh caught prey. All the world was a fire and she was caught in the middle of its blaze—

"—wake—wake up!"

Back and forth the boiling water washed her body. She tried to fight but it had taken her, sapped from her all her strength. Still it played with her.

"Wake up!"

Simsa saw a face above her—large as the moon, round—with two dark pits for eyes, a mouth come to suck her out of the water. Still, there would be no safety in that mouth—only another kind of torment—

"Wake up!"

The huge face receded, became one she could remember dimly. She blinked, the water had made her sight hazy. She—

No dream — no fire — the hands of the off-worlder were on her shoulders shaking her. She gaped at him a moment and then pulled away.

"You must have had a dream to end all dreams — on the dark side," he commented as he sat back on his heels. "Here, take this." He held out the pannikan she had last used to ease the thirst of the zorsals. "Take it," he urged again when she had not put up her hand.

This was the valley still and the heat lapped around her. But there was something curious, too. It was as if from time to time she saw one thing across another — the valley clear, then veiled by a topling tower and a pool into which fear was driving her, death before her, behind her and all around.

"Drink!" He moved, was at her side, his arm firmly about her shoulders, so that she was supported against the swing of the sickening visions, one upon the other. The edge of the pannikan against her sore lips was a small pain, yet it, more than his voice, broke up that last vestige of her dream.

She did not question that the pannikan was near full. The water was warm and slightly bitter, but she drank it all thirstily, allowing him to hold the cup until the end.

He settled her shoulders back against the hamper from which she could hear the small panting gasps of the zorsals. They needed tending, but her head felt so light and queer she could not force herself to move — not yet.

Instead, not understanding what he did, she watched the off-worlder pick up a small vial from the rock by his knee, measure three drops from it into the water he poured with such care. Stoppering the vial and replacing it in his pouch he lifted the pannikan as one who was meeting a friend in an inn, made a gesture in her direction, and sipped slowly at the portion he had allowed himself. Still over the rim of the cup he studied her so intently that at last she moved a little, uncomfortable under so keen and searching a gaze.

"I did have a bad dream," she said, as if she must justify whatever she had done to so engage his concern. "It—it was a part of this . . . somehow."

She raised her hand and let the ring tower stand high. "Fire in the sky and a falling tower—and I jumped into a pool but the water—was boiling."

"Lady Simsa," he still kept that courteous form of speech which had so irritated her—though she would not give him the satisfaction of hearing her protest against what must be a subtle kind of mockery, "have you ever heard among your people of strange talents which some may have? Have you known, or heard, of one who can take a thing into his or her hands and read then the past through which it has come?"

For some odd reason she was beginning to feel stronger, more alert than she had in days. She straightened up from leaning against the hamper, reached behind her to tend the zorsals. What he said—could any one believe that such things were? No, he was not testing her by some new folly that to him *might* be the truth—on another world.

"No," she answered shortly. She did not like at all this talk of things so strange. All her life she had been burdened by her difference in color, in kind, from anyone in the Burrows, any she had seen in Kuxortal. She had done the best that she could to conceal that difference—which was of the body. Now he spoke of worse differences—for, to her, that talk appeared more dangerous than any mirror image of herself.

"Such things are known. Those who have a gift such as that are recognized among my people, trained to use it—"

"I have no such 'gift'!" Gift indeed, it would have been only one more thing which would have set her apart. "If you are through with that," she nodded to the pannikan, "the zorsals must be tended."

Unless, she thought, with a sudden stab of fear he might consider the creatures useless baggage, believe that the water she must have to keep them alive would be better used to continue their own existence.

However, he did not protest. In fact she noted that the portion he poured out was certainly higher in the cup than that which he had taken for himself. One by one she brought the limp and drooping creatures out of their shelter, induced them to drink, laid them carefully, their feet under them, their wings smooth against their backs, on the lid of the hamper.

She became aware as she did so that her store of new energy was growing. In spite of the heat which lingered here she had found some reserve within herself which gave her the power to move with more strength than she had known since they left the shoreside. The cliff held shadows now and the off-worlder was settling, with extreme care, the magic lift box in the center of the carrier which arose with something close to a leap and then floated near his shoulder level until he dragged it down and had Simsa sit on the edge and hand him the hampers and the rest of the gear when he called for them, he making very certain that each was put in an exact place, though she could see no real purpose in his care.

They ate, and now the zorsals were fanning their wings, their heads raised, hooting a little back and forth.

Simsa, as Thom tied the last cord, lifted Zass to her shoulder ready to move out. Thus once more they began the journey along what seemed, from all Simsa could spy ahead, to remain an endless chasm, the walls, the footage no different than those they had passed the night before.

Their journey started with the coming of dusk, Thom again in the lead, Simsa swinging from side to side behind, her attention for the carrier when its sway might bring it into contact with the rocks. It rode she believed a little higher above the ground than it had the first night of their journey. Perhaps the water and food they had taken, small as that quantity was, had made the difference.

It was a weary business, her own small surprise was that she found herself stepping out so briskly after the long baking of the day, able to move quickly to fend off the carrier from some obstruction at need. With the downing of the sun the zorsals once more took to the air, Zass screaming harshly after them, as if to make sure she would be entitled to some portion of any prey this achingly barren land might yield.

Once more they halted at intervals, and the second time they did Thom asked suddenly:

"How do you feel?"

There was a note in his voice which alerted the girl. Almost as if he expected her to report some measure of difficulty—because of her dream? She shied away from such questions as he had asked her about the strange "talent," as he had named it, which some off-worlders believed in.

"I am able to go where you lead," she retorted sharply. "All have dreams they would rather not remember by re-telling over and over—or are your people so different that they are not troubled by such?"

"It is not your dream." The shadows in the cut lay between them, so thick a curtain she could not see his face except as a lighter patch in the general gloom, for the light which showed them their way and which hung from his belt, was now, as he sat eating, directed on the slightly swaying carrier. "I must tell you what I did, for the time may come when it is necessary that you know what to do. In this," he tapped his pouch—"the liquid you saw me add to the water before I drank—is a stimulant, a distillation of several, as you would call them, medicines which strengthen the body, clear the mind. One cannot use much, nor too often. It is meant to carry one through such trials as we have had to meet. I did not know whether it would aid you—I had to take the chance. You—you were far gone."

She chewed upon that information along with the piece of concentrated food she held and tried not to smell as she ate.

"You could have slain me so." She hoped her voice was as steady as she wanted it to be.

"Yes, I might have killed you."

Simsa considered that. He was a truth speaker, this off-worlder. At first her anger flared up, but she would not allow that to cloud her wits as badly as those half visions she had seen upon awakening. He had taken a chance, and it had worked. She knew she was stronger, more alert, better able to carry on. When she thought back to the heat and torment of the day behind she wondered if she *could* have summoned the power, even if she had had the will, to start forth again on the journey unaided.

"It did not." She would not allow him to know if she cared one way or another. They were nothing to each other. Just as she had been nothing to anyone since Ferwar had died. For a moment or two another part of her was surprised even at that fleeting thought; Simsa need not be anything to or for anyone but herself! .

"Simsa," it was the first time he had not added "lady" to her name, but spoke it as if she were one with him, equal and a part of the same venture, "whose House gave you birth?"

"House?" She laughed scornfully and Zass gave her instant answer, querulously. "When did a Burrower have a 'House' to boast of? We may know our mothers—some our fathers also—but beyond that . . ." she shrugged, even though he might not see that gesture. "No, we count no further."

"And your mother?" he persisted past all common courtesy—though she had believed that he at least owed her that much.

She could say anything—that she was some drop child even of a Guild Woman and he could not now name her liar. Why should she? It was easier in one way to answer with the truth.

"You know as much as I do. I remember rolling in the dirt of Ferwar's Burrow—no farther back than that. But I was not any fruit of her body. She was past the age of spawning when I was born." Deliberately she used the harsh terms of the Burrowers, stripping away all the fine talk such as he might be used to. "Perhaps I was a heap child."

"A heap child?"

"One thrown on the refuse heaps and left for the scavengers." Still deliberately she set herself as low as this world would rate her. Taking, for a reason she could not understand, a perverse pleasure in doing so. "Perhaps

Ferwar gleaned me there. She was one curious enough to bring back strange things. Do you not carry with you even now some of her finds? I am not as remarkable perhaps as your things of this—this X-Arth—but it would well be that to the Old One I had some value."

"At least I had such to her as she grew older. She was troubled with much pain in her joints, and became so crippled that it was hard for her to go either burrowing or comb the rubbish. I was too small to carry large things but she always said I had good eyes. I am lucky, too—or was—" She thought she could not claim that her present state was a fortunate one. "I found some of the Old One's good pieces. And I had Zass; no one else had ever thought of trying to tame a zorsal and then loan its services for hire."

"Yes."

She wished that she could see his expression now. He had agreed with her in a single word. Oddly enough she would have liked him to be more astounded. But then, how could an off-worlder know what it was like to live in the Burrows? To live a life in which one existed on what all in Kuxortal threw away, or lost, or had hidden and forgotten, long before one was born?

"There were none there who were like you—with your hair—your skin?"

"None!" she did not know whether to be proud of that but she made her answer ring proudly enough. "They called me Shadow—I need only bind up my hair, use the soot from the cooking pot on my brows and lashes and I had become part of the night itself. Also, Ferwar warned me to be careful. She said there were those who might use my strangeness for trading—making me part of what they would sell. I learned to hide much of what I am. That was useful many times over." She allowed herself a small laugh but did not hear him equal it.

"So none saw you to remark upon your difference. And this Old One of yours believed it could be a danger—?"

Simsa could not understand why he harped so on her appearance. She was strange—but there were many in the Burrows who were the result of hasty and near forgotten coupling between strangers. She had once been envious of Lanwor who had been bought from his "father" (if Qualt was his father) because of his extraordinarily long arms. He had been taken into the Thieves' Guild, which was an upward advance in the world. She had sometimes wondered whether Ferwar had ever been approached—a small child who could fade into the dark and be a part of it should have had a price also. Was that why the Old One has so often harped upon concealment? By the time Ferwar was dead she was too independent, too old, to be trained by their harsh and rigid underrules.

"Not many ever saw me when I was older." Thinking back she saw that that was true. "Not as I was. The Old One put a cap on me when I went out foraging. She did not want to shave my head, I don't know why. It was easier to go capped than to wash color out in the river. Then she began rather to send me at night and taught me how to go unseen. There were those in strange places with whom she dealt in some manner—I never understood how or why—I took things to them secretly and brought other packages in return."

It seemed that he had now run out of questions for he was busy with the water jar they had opened earlier, dealing out their shares. Having drunk down the flat tasting warmth of that, she had a question in turn:

"And what of *your* House, starman? Are you a lord's son that you have been free to flit from world to world as Zass's sons can alight on one rock and then another? How great are your courts, and how many gather to call aloud your clan name in the dawn?"

Now he did laugh. "Our customs are not quite as those of Kuxortal. No one of us sets up such a household of kin. There were my parents but they are dead long since. My brother was the older, therefore the head of our House, as you would name it. We have one sister. She is wed to a star captain and lives ever traveling. That life is to her liking, but I have not seen her for many years. My brother is a man respected by men of learning, and, to a part, I share his teaching and his tastes. We were engaged on different projects when I heard of his disappearance here. Then I knew that I must come and seek him. So I went to my chief—the Histor-Techneer Zashion himself—and I said this I must do. He gave me leave and I came on the first ship I could find which was to make landing here. On the way I learned from tapes what my brother was seeking and what might be before me. Hence my bringing of such as the nullifier, though that was unlawful. But I could not see why once I arrived the questions I asked brought such hesitations to the very people who should be the first to give me full aid.

"After all it would be to their advantage to help a Histor-Techneer of the League. If they feared that we were such as to steal ancient treasure they had our bonds and the assurance of the League itself that we were nothing of the kind."

"This League of yours," Simsa had given Zass a full half of her share of cake, having heard no hunting calls from the two who had taken to the sky overhead—"where is its city?"

"City? There is no one city. The League is a union of worlds, many worlds, like your union of Guild Masters in Kuxortal."

"But it has," she pointed out triumphantly, "no guild guards here has it? How think you that any Guild Lord would take seriously the word of a man whose guards he could not see every day, whose house badge was not displayed openly? Your League is far away, they are here. They will do as they please and see no reason why that should not be so."

She thought he sighed, but she could not be sure. He did not break the silence again. She had begun to lose quite a bit of her recent awe of him. He possessed such tools as the box which lightened a load until it was no real burden at all, a light which burned without consuming anything as a lamp did oil, but in the affairs of men he was less than any child of the Burrows on his first lone seeking and shifting.

The zorsals killed and again brought a portion to their dam. Then they arose and whirled away before Simsa could lay any command upon them. It was a night without moonlight, and she had not seen in which direction they flew. She only hoped they would come home before the rise of the pitiless sun.

There was a grayness in the sky when, for the first time, Simsa became aware that the flooring of the cut was changing, deepening. Also it was smoother, here were fewer rock falls about which they must guide the carrier. At the same time she heard an exclamation from her companion. He had halted abruptly, the carrier actually sliding a little ahead with the momentum of his steady pull, to strike against his hip. Simsa stepped to one side to see the better.

They had certainly come to the end of this valley. Before them, as forbidding as any wall set about an armed keep such as the river people spoke of in the far places, was a cliff, which went up and up. She saw Thom detach the light giver from his belt, hold that at angle so that its beam illumined the rise. To her it looked as if the light failed before the top, if this wall had any top at all. Certainly it must be twice the height of the cliffs which had been on either side during their whole journey up from the sea.

"I think," Thom said, as calmly as if he were not staring straight at what the girl saw now only as disaster, "that we have reached our goal—this must be the beginning of the Hard Hills."

Simsa dropped down. That energy which had sustained her through the night might have washed out of her in the same moment as she realized the meaning of his words.

"We cannot climb that." Oh, there were fissures and holes which she could see in the light, but they dare not attempt such a feat until day would make all clear, and with day would come the sun which would crisp them as they struggled.

"Then we shall find another way—"

She would have hurled a stone at him had there been any to hand, but this way was barren of all but gravel. He was so calm, always so very sure that there was no problem which would not yield to him.

"Your lifting box might carry Zass," she returned, refusing to let her irritation break through. "Us it could not manage."

However, it was as if he had not listened to her at all,

instead he asked a question which half buried her comment: "How much communication do you have with these zorsals of yours? I know they will come to your call, and that you could set them in Gathar's warehouse to keep the vermin down. But can you impress upon them some other task?"

"What kind of a task?" She was smoothing Zass's fur and felt that the antennae on the zorsal's head were not only completely uncurled, but slanting in the direction of the off-worlder, quivering slightly, which she knew meant that the creature was concentrating. Could Zass grasp the sense of what he said to the extent that she knew he was speaking of her and her two sons?

"To make it to the top of this." He let his light flicker up and down the surface of the cliff as far as the beam would reach. "We would need a rope. That we have—or will when I do a little work upon the lashings. Could your zorsals be sent to carry such aloft, put it around some outcrop there and return with the end to us or—"

His suggestion was drowned out by a scream of rage from the sky. Down into the beam of the light came one of the zorsals, and it was pursued by something else—a thing which, to Simsa, might have flown out of a dream as harrowing as that which had held her before waking last evening.

This monster was like a long thin rope in itself, and it would seem that its other end was safely rooted somehow, for they could only see the forepart of the head—that which was all gaping jaws and needle teeth, darting and striving to strike at the zorsal. Into the beam of light in which that attack was so clear to view, flew the second zorsal who flung itself, to fasten on the darting head just behind the jaws. Three long clawed paws found anchorage and held, the fourth ripped busily back and forth across the large, seemingly lidless, eyes of the monster.

Seeing its attacker so engaged the other zorsal turned swiftly and flew back and forth while the monster apparently, so mad with rage it did not realize just which was its attacker, kept trying to snap at the second, leaving the other to inflict continued punishment.

Both eyes were bloody pits now and an outflung paw had ripped a length from the long, darting tongue. Simsa had always known that the zorsals were killers and that they took a certain enjoyment in their slaying—unless they killed quickly for food alone. But she had never guessed they would tackle so large a prey, or that they were keen witted enough to fight it in the only way possible for them to survive.

8.

From Simsa's shoulder Zass set up a clamor, flexing her good wing, flapping uselessly with the other as if she fought to take to the air and be a part of that battle. The zorsal who had fastened on the head of the monster still raked that viciously. Now his brother darted in and sank both claws and teeth into the scaled throat as the embattled creature tossed its head wildly, trying to shake off its tormentor. There was a gash opened across the column of the body. From that spurted a thick, yellowish stream of blood which bespattered the stone, flew in great gouts through the air, so that the two below leaped back and away to escape the shower.

Both zorsals kept to their attack and then the great jawed head flapped in such a loose manner Simsa thought that the neck must be near bitten through. The struggles became only a jerking of the dangling length of the body, while the zorsals settled on the head, tore and feasted.

Thom turned to Simsa. "What is this?"

She shook her head wordlessly. Though she had never thought to be squeamish (no Burrower could be that) the ferocity of the zorsals and the threat of the huge thing itself had shaken her so that she felt weak enough to put

out a hand and steady herself against the carrier. Only that bobbed so under her weight that she was near thrown off balance.

Thom went as close to the cliff side as he could. He had unfastened in some fashion the light from his belt and now he turned that up, holding its beam directly on the thing and the feeding zorsals. Simsa detached the complaining Zass from her shoulder, put the creature on the sled, and, trying to avoid the smears and still falling gouts of blood, worked her way to join him. One of the hunters now dropped, with a beating of wings, a dripping piece of scaled flesh in its forefeet to present this offering to Zass, whose cries had grown louder and louder.

Simsa gasped. The light showed a length of still slightly twisting body which was far larger than her own height even added to Thom's. Yet they could not see the end of it, for, though the beam cut acros the top of that wall, the body must still be longer, it fell over the edge like a rope.

They really did not need the beam to show it now. In the coming dawn it fell very clear against the stone. A rope Simsa had first compared it to in her mind—only this thing of flesh and bone was as thick as about a handful of ropes twisted all together. Thom switched off his off-world lamp and moved back again.

"We have found our way—" he said slowly.

The zorsals had near finished their grisly feast. The one who had attacked the monster first dropped to join Zass on the carrier to lick busily at its fur, sucking each claw in turn. While the brother tore loose another mouthful, brought that down to sample in satiated small bits. Only a near stripped skull swung there now.

"What would you do?" Simsa watched Thom free a coil of rope from the carrier, busy himself making a noose at one end of it.

"Our ladder aloft—" He waved his hand at the dangling dead thing, "if it is well held above. We shall see."

He whirled his noose about his head, keeping careful grip on the cord of which it was a part. Three ties he made before it encircled that picked skull and he settled the rope tightly in place with a sharp jerk, as if he had often used this trick.

"Now—" pulling the rope taught, he stepped back— "let us see."

She watched his shoulders tense, could understand the steady pull he was exerting. The girl reached down and caught at the loose end of the cord, added her strength to his for this test.

The cord slipped a little in the mangled part, then caught, and, though Simsa was bending all the force she could and believed that the off-worlder did also, it felt as secure as if the rope was fast tied around some spine of rock.

"I shall go—" he told her. "When I get to the top, lash the end of the cord I shall drop about your waist and follow—but bring this also with you."

He was busy once again with more rope, adding a long length to that with which he had towed the carrier. Having tested his knots he stood over that wonder box to make some small adjustment. The carrier suddenly jumped aloft, sending Zass fluttering toward Simsa with a loud scream, the other two zorsals winging into the air. Now their transport floated at shoulder level with Thom.

"This causes a greater drain," she did not know whether he was speaking now to her or merely thinking aloud, "but it will help."

The longer draw rope he now tossed to her while he

faced the cliff side, the end of the climbing rope made fast about him, his face a mask of determination. Simsa watched him carefully. Though his hands were on the rope and his shoulders showed the strain he put upon them, he also used any toe hold on the face of the cliff which he could find.

The day was coming fast. Thom had reached the gory head of the monster, shifted his hold from the rope to the thing's body. The two zorsals who could fly were following him up, screaming all the way. Simsa turned quickly now to Zass and made the spitting, excited creature let herself be stuffed into the baggy front of the girl's jacket.

Somehow she did not want to watch Thom climb the dangling body. She was fighting nausea, trying to keep out of her mind the knowledge that she must do this in turn.

Only . . , she had to see!

It seemed that in those few moment during which she had turned away, he had won a distance she could not have thought possible. One arm swung out, a hand had cupped over the edge of the cliff. She saw him hang so for a moment which was lifted out of normal time. Then he had pulled himself up—his head and shoulders disappeared, he must be wriggling so on his stomach—he was gone!

Simsa shut her eyes for a moment and then opened them again. She found that she had grasped the belt about her, the rope of the carrier which she had tied there, with such force that her fingers ached. Swallowing hard, she made herself look up.

The off-worlder had returned to the edge of the cliff but now he was facing outward, looking down to her.

Though he must be still lying flat.

"This—about you—" He tossed another length of rope, which confused her, but that she must trust him she understood.

She leaped and caught the dangling end, felt that it gave so she could pull it down, tie it around her beside that attached to the carrier. The rope grew taut and she realized that he must be adding power to raise it.

Using the same actions as she had observed, she set her bundled feet wherever she might discover some hold, drew herself up, knew he was also taking much of the strain from her. The worst of her nightmare did not come, she could hold to the rope he had dropped, did not have to climb over the bloody head of the creature. Though once past that point, she put out a hand now and then against its scaled body and found the rough surface of that, while it abraded her hands, was secure enough to keep away the worst fear of the rope slipping through her clutch.

It seemed that she was trying to reach the top of a mountain and her struggle had no end. Already the heat of the day struck against her back. Twice she had to fend herself away from the wall lest Zass be crushed. Then she heard a voice call:

"Your hand—reach to me with your hand!"

She groped upward blindly, felt his fingers close about hers. In a moment she cried out:

"Wait—there is Zass—"

However, the zorsal was already on the move on her own behalf. She pulled out of the pocket front, flapped, and now spun out to catch the rope for herself, crawling up and over Simsa's hands. Then the girl herself was brought up, scraping over stone, to roll out on a surface where the sand rose in puffs to make her cough. Before she could straighten up she felt hands about her middle tugging at the rope.

"Up with it—"

Hardly aware of what she did, only that she must do it, Simsa did not try to get up any further than her knees. She caught at the carrier rope which had swung back and forth across her and began to pull. The off-worlder was standing now, only more rigid with the strain of bringing that heavy burden.

The girl had no time to look around until that drew level with them, the starman's box keeping it under control. Together they worked to swing it in, scrambling back to give it room well beyond the cliff edge. Thom went at once to the box, but Simsa sat back now to survey where all this effort had brought them.

Immediately before her and reaching well back into a tangle of rocks and thorn studded, dried vegetation, bleached to the color of bones was the rest of the body of the monster. Here it was rounded to at least ten times its circumference at the point of the long neck. However, it displayed no sign of feet—tapering again so that the portion hidden by the covering from which it must have earlier crawled, was slimmed down like the tail of one of those small things the zorsals had fed upon during their night forage. She could not understand what had kept it so adherent to the rock that they had been able to use as a ladder without bringing the whole weight of it down upon them.

Apparently this puzzle interested Thom also, for, once he was sure that their carrier was intact, its cargo undisturbed, he went to the side of the thing and strove to roll it over. However, it remained as tight to the rock as if it were indeed a part of the ground. Finally he used a piece of stone to pry up a portion of the body so Simsa caught sight of a pallid half ring of flesh, before he was forced to let the weight fall again.

"Suckers I think," he commented. "What is it called?"

She shook her head in bewilderment.

"I do not know, nor have I ever heard of such before."

"Well," he half turned to face east, his hands on his hips, his head up, "there are the Hard Hills! Let us hope that such as this are not plentiful here." He prodded the carcass with the toe of his boot.

Simsa looked ahead. She had thought that the cliff up which they had just fought their way was a barrier. Only, from what she could see now, it was just the beginning. Hills? No—these were sky scraping monsters of earth and stone. Still they held one promise for any who had fought across the desert land—they gave foothold here and there to growth of some sort—sere and sun-browned now perhaps—but it had lived. Where that lived there must be water, perhaps game.

Heartened by that thought Simsa got to her feet. They were still in the sun's full heat. Yet surely in the broken country ahead they could find shelter for the day—and perhaps even more. She said as much and the off-worlder nodded.

"We have have to do some more climbing," he pointed out, "but you are right—where there is growth there must be water. And, in spite of the evil name of this place, I think we may find it more welcoming than the desert. But first we shall camp—and soon."

They were still in a depression between crumbling banks of sun-baked earth and long dead brush. Thom speculated as to whether they were not still following the path of a long-dry water course, and that the cliff up which they had come had constituted a falls. There was a lot of sand through which they slipped and slid, sometimes ankle deep, hurrying now, while surveying the way ahead in hope of a place to shelter before the punishing heat of the day struck them down with exhaustion.

The dried up water course took a slow curve to the left and there was a rise of stone on one bank, half undermined, so that some had fallen over in a rough tumble which nearly barricaded the way. Thom swung toward those and Simsa, at her old place of keeping the carrier steady, padded behind. Now, as they drew closer, she could see that those were no stones heaped by some whim of nature. These had been trimmed, set, and used, even though years, wind, and sand had eroded them into their present anonymous heaping.

Among those fallen blocks they found their shelter, a darkish hole which was still sheltered by half an archway. Inside it were steps leading down. Thom switched on his light once again. Here was welcoming cool shadow. The zorsals honked and spiralled ahead eagerly. Simsa caught at the off-worlder's sleeve.

"Wait—let them search. If there is life denned below—" She could not help but think of the dead monster and that just such a hole as this could offer such a creature a home.

He halted, his head up, and she knew that, just as she did, he was listening. The zorsal calls sounded from below, oddly hollow, stronger as if some chance made those sounds monsters of *their* kind. Zass, from her seat on the carrier, thrust forward her head, her antennae advanced, her thin lips almost invisible, as she showed all her pointed teeth.

Simsa sniffed, trying to draw into her lungs enough of any odor which might lie below to judge what they could have to face. There was none of the smell of the Burrows, the mustiness of close and none too clean living. When the zorsals did not return to raise any alarm, she nodded to her companion.

"I think that nothing waits here—nothing living."

Though falls of dressed, if much wind-worn stone, half blocked that entrance so that scaling the carrier across it took patience and skill on both their parts, the stairs beyond that were reasonably clear. These were broad and the rises were shorter, so that to descend was easy enough. Save that they went on and on as if there were no end and that this long forsaken building had been raised on a foundation of long forgotten predecessors, as Kuxortal had been.

There was the relief, that, the farther they descended, the cooler it became. Zass still hunched forward listening. From what seemed very far away Simsa could still hear the cries of the other zorsals. In the dark they always hooted and cried continually, since, she had discovered, something in their own screeching made it easier for them to elude any obstruction which even their dark-piercing eyes might not be able to see.

Thom had once more switched on his belt light. When she turned her head a little and looked back over her own shoulder, the girl could see that the opening above had shrunken greatly. Yet the steps continued.

They stopped once, drank sparingly and ate, seated on one steps, shoulder to shoulder. Simsa inspected the supplies left. They could keep on going as long as they had water, but there would come an end if they could not add to their food, and where, in this parched land, might they find any such? The scaled things the zorsals relished? She gagged at the sudden memory of the huge monster, now dangling dead across the cliff edge, which came far too clearly into mind. She had eaten much in the past which any dweller of the upper city would have disdained, but not that!

"Where do we go?" she asked, though she knew that he could have no better answer for her than some guess which she might make for herself.

"This might well be the remains of some outpost. That being so there could also be a linkage by passageway to another and larger fortification beyond. In times of war such would provide a secret way of supply."

"Why so deep?" Again she squeezed around on the wide step. That opening so far behind them now was made so small by distance that she could raise her hand and cover it with her thumb. Still the stairway went on down and down, for Thom had gone to his knees, and, having deliberately taken the light from his belt, swept the ray back and forth over what was only an endless stair without a break.

Her legs ached. They had traveled all through the night and she could not tell how far they were into the next day now. Surely they must have a time to rest, and soon.

The off-worlder might have picked up that thought from out of her head for now he said:

"Let us go five tens farther. Then if there is no end as yet we shall rest."

With a sigh Simsa pulled herself up. The wrappings about her feet had worn very thin. Sooner or later she would have to use her belt knife to cut strips from her coat to replace those. The only good thing was that they were no longer blasted by that heavy punishment from the sun. In fact . . .

Simsa's head came up. Once more she drew into her lungs as deep a breath as she could.

"Damp!" She had cried that so loud that, as had the early calls of the zorsals, the word was echoed hollowly back to her from down in the darkness, as if a line of Simsas stationed along the steps passed such a discovery from one to the next.

Thom, his face only a blur in the reflection of the lamp, looked toward her.

"Yes," he agreed.

"Water?" Her fatigue pushed aside now, she got to her feet eagerly. Zass's antennae had curled slightly, while they rested and she had crunched with grunts of protest part of Simsa's food. Now she sidled towards the front of the carrier, both her sense organs extended to their farthest limit. From deep in her furred throat came chirps of impatience.

Still they descended. When they came to the fifty-step level Thom had set for them, he flashed the beam along the walls. There were patches of damp, giving nourishment to queer growths of pallid white which formed as not quite regular balls, extending thread-like filaments outward to attach to each of the slimy looking sections of damp.

Simsa disliked the look of these and made certain that if she put out a hand to steady herself she would not touch one.

"Let us go on!" Though her whole body was one ache, she could not stay surrounded by this place which worked upon her inborne sense of danger to such an extent.

Thom needed no urging. They had gone down perhaps

five more of the wide and shallow steps when he uttered an exclamation.

The light hit upon, lanced along a level way. They had reached the end of the stairway at long last! Here the damp was heavy but the air itself was not noisome nor dead. Simsa whistled, and from not too far away came an answer. Then one of the zorsals winged into the path of the light, circled about her head.

"Look!" There was no mistaking the water sleeked fur on his forelimbs. The creature had very lately found a source of that great enough to soak as the zorsals were apt to do during the heat of the dry season—spending hours supine in the bowls of water that those who valued them always provided.

Tired as they were the sight of the zorsal, who uttered small cries of what Simsa well recognized as contentment, urged them on, and at this level they fell into a stumbling trot. Zass's demands set up an echoing of squawking which near covered the thud of their own footfalls.

Though moisture and the unpleasant growths still studded the walls, there was no wet underfoot. The girl noted that at the base of each wall was a shallow trench which perhaps was meant to carry off any runnels the plants had not sucked away.

Their beam of light suddenly was snapped off. Simsa let out a small cry of which she was ashamed a moment later. To allow the off-worlder to know that she feared the dark in any way was a humiliation. Then she could see his reason. Not far ahead, there was a haze of light, not as strong as that of his lamp, but sufficient to provide a guide.

As they approached the girl noted that the source of the light seemed to lie to their left, being much stronger there. Then they came to an abrupt end to the passage, with a doorway on one side through which the haze came.

For haze it was, not the clean-cut beam of any torch or lamp. The effect was more as if they were advancing into a fog made of small particles of dim light which swam, gathered, and then split apart again. That zorsal who had circled overhead, now gave an alert squawk, and flew straight into the curtain which closed about him so that only muffled cries resounded.

"Slow—watch the footing—"

Simsa did not need such a warning from her companion. She had already cut her trot to a walk. The fog-stuff was wet, like sea spume, save that it did not carry the sting of salt in it. As it closed about her so closely that she was aware of Thom as only a bulk moving through the mist, she felt thick moisture gather on her skin. This was like stepping down into one of those baths which she had experienced only twice in her life, when she had had a chance to gather enough extra silver bits to visit the one open to the most humble of Kuxortal.

The damp mist, though, had none of the strong perfumes which were a part of the city baths and which Simsa had never cared for. But she felt as if her skin, so dried and lacking in water's touch for many days, was growing softer, that her body, more than her mouth, was absorbing what she had lacked for so long.

As she had done in the heat of the day she pulled at the belting of her jacket, opening that wide so that the touch of this fog, so soft, so healing (for it seemed thus to her) could reach all the areas of skin she was able to bare.

Where this mist arose from she could not tell, for there was no longer any sight of walls, only pavement underfoot, the outline of Thom, and behind him the carrier which she no longer had to push this way and that to keep on the level and moving. Zass had flopped over, belly up, her head stretched to the full extent of her long neck, that she might so expose all of her body that she could. After the burning of the desert this was like standing under the sky in the first of the wet-season rains while those drops still fell slowly and gently, and one was not yet battered by any wind.

Then the haze began to clear. Patches thickened, appeared to swirl this way and that out of their path, as if the fog itself held a sense of being, and would not impede their passage. Thus they came out of one last pocket into the full open.

Simsa gave a small sigh. Her feet folded under her and she dropped, her hands plunging into powdery sand or earth so soft that it deadened instantly all the jar of her fall. She slipped into it, her hands unable to find any firm floor to support her, and lay, her cheek pillowed on one crooked arm, surveying what small bit of this place she could see.

That it was totally unlike any site she had ever heard described by the most far roving trader, bore no mention in even legends, was very clear. They had come into a space large enough to be as wide as one of the market squares of the upper city. In shape it was as circular as if they were caught up in the cup some giant, grown beyond human reckoning, had carelessly set down.

The outer walls were formed by the fog-mist which constantly moved, thickened, lightened, but never allowed one a clear view of what lay beyond. While sand in which she rested, feeling as if all energy had seeped out of her forever, was not white-grey like the fog, rather it held the glint of true silver—as if that most precious of metals (as far as the Burrowers were concerned) had been ground and reground until it was as fine as the flour from which the upper city baked its festival bread. Simsa sifted the powder through her fingers and was sure, that, though there was no sun to awaken any answering glitter, this was truly some precious stuff.

It spilled in an even rim about a regularly shaped pool. The water of that (if it were water) was a clouded pale silver-white—such a color as she had seen before. Her hand fell back into the sand, and she saw the ring again. Slowly, because her mind seemed so bemused by the waves of weariness which swept over her now, Simsa made the comparison. This pool was the very shade of the gem in the circlet she wore.

Simsa lay still. Zass hopped from the carrier. Using her one good wing as she was used to doing when there was need, she thrust the leather tip of that deep into the sand, leaned on it as she purposefully made for the water which lay so silent, nothing disturbing its gem-smooth surface.

Could she depend upon the zorsal's instinct, so much stronger than those of any of her own species, to judge that the opaque liquid was harmless? The girl tried to sit up, uttered a call which was only a soft murmur in her throat. Zass paid no heed, her dogged purpose was plain, as she scuffed through the silver sand and at last reached the water's edge.

With a small croak she gave a last hop which launched her out into the pool. She did not sink, rather she floated as if that water might have substance enough to support her small body. The good wing was spread wide, the other as far as she could bend it. She had lifted her head to turn her long neck and rest her jaw on the edge of the good wing. Her large eyes closed, and it was apparent that she was at peace, experiencing now one of the highest pleasures of her own kind.

There was a stir at Simsa's other side. She was too drained to turn her head. Then into the line of her vision the off-worlder came. He had unsealed his garment, was stripping it down from his body with a purpose which Simsa could guess. Again a faint stirring of protest tried to raise her and failed.

Whiter than the mist walling them was his body. He looked somehow larger, more impressive than he had when clothed. Now he stepped across the narrow bridge of sand, turning aside to allow Zass full room to float in comfort. Rather than diving he seemed to fall forward, as if his action had been the last surge of what energy he still possessed. Slowly his body turned, sinking no further for his bulk than Zass had. He floated, face upward, his eyes slowly closing, his breast rising and falling as one who lay in the best slumber of the night.

Simsa watched and a longing grew in her. Whatever her two companions found there—that she must have also. She discovered herself crying weakly because she could not join them. From her tears and despair she sank into a dark which closed deeply about her.

9.

She was lying on such a bed as she had never dreamed might exist, one which accepted her slight body with a cool adjustment for every bone and muscle so that she was a part of the bed and its comfort wooed her to sleep. Still, somewhere deep within her there was a nagging need for movement, for awareness of more than that lazy, insidious comfort, something which urged her back into the world.

Simsa opened her eyes. She was looking up at a rolling, ever-changing, slow-billowing of what might be cloud. Never in her life had she felt so content, so unaware of her body—as if that had been lulled into a peaceful slumber in which all pain and fatigue had been lost. She raised one arm slowly. For it seemed that, while caught in this delicious languor, she could not, nor did she need, to make any swift gesture. Her body moved also, even as her arm came into view. Whatever she lay on was not solid—

The slow languor vanished. Simsa slapped with both arms, rolled over, and her head and face went under. Startled, fear pulling her body taut, she strove to climb out, to fight back against what held her.

"Wait—lie still."

Simsa thoroughly frightened now splashed the harder.

Then her head was pulled back by an ungentle hold upon her hair. She rolled once more so that her face was uppermost and she could breathe. The hold on her did not loosen, instead she was being towed through this stuff which was far thicker than any true water. She opened her mouth and screamed, all the sweet contentment of moments earlier gone.

Then her head was dropped to lie on a support which was firm, leaving her face well out of the water. She reached out, half expecting only water, but her hands discovered that she now lay only part way in the pool, her legs still trailing outward. By using her arms and hands she was able to work her body up into a place where the powder-sand was near as soft a cushion as the pool's contents had been.

Simsa sat up. Against the silver of the sand, the opaque glory of the pool, her dark body was in vivid contrast. She was not wet. Her skin where she had won out into the air was damp, but it seemed either that moisture drained at once from her, or else was drawn as quickly off by the air. Even the mass of her hair, as she raised her hands to push it away from her brow and throw it back over her shoulders, was far less damp than it had been when she had come in from an early morning foraging in the dew which lay on the scrub growth of the river banks around Kuxortal.

If the water was not wet—it had performed something else which was to her comfort—that comfort which she had almost lost as her first bemused awakening. Her skin was firm, and *clean* as she could never remember it being before. Now she wriggled her feet. Freed of the clumsy wrappings, the worn-out sandals, there were no bruises, no small pains of scrapes and abrasions. She had a body renewed, made whole, free and well.

She drew her hands slowly down that body, over her small, high breasts, over her narrow waist, her thin, scarcely rounded thighs. Her own fingers moving thus made her feel as if she were being stroked lovingly, given a pleasure so full that she answered with a crooning murmur deep in her throat, even as Zass answered when she was scratched along jaw line, and slowly, carefully, at the base of her antennae.

All the hunger and thirst which Simsa had brought here were dim memories. The desert journey was something that had happened to someone else. The girl surveyed her hand dreamily, and on her thumb the ring had moved about, the plain band facing the palm, the tower standing tall and proud. She was right—the rich, opaque shade of the unknown jewel was the same color as the liquid from which she had just come. She laughed aloud. Her feeling of well being was as if she had drunk a full draft of rich wine. Once one of the Burrowers, seeking to curry favor with Ferwar when the Old One was ill with that pain which racked her limbs, had brought a bottle over which the woman had chuckled.

Ferwar had measured out its contents in hardly more than sips. Then she had fallen asleep and Simsa, greatly daring, had taken the small portion which was left from the Old One's last pouring. The wine had been cool in her mouth, warm in her middle. She had felt for a while as if she so wished she might take wing to seek the upper air, as free as a zorsal in the night. This same freedom was in her now. She threw wide her arms, and trilled the notes which summoned her creatures.

They came, beating their way out of the mist, to whirl about her head. As she turned to watch them she was aware that her hair lifted somewhat of its own accord. That vigorous life now within her seemed to give the damp locks freedom also. There was another call and floating across the pool came Zass.

Only there was something odd about the zorsal. She rested breast down on the surface, not sinking in—her good wing spread wide. Her good wing—? Simsa stared, startled out of her concentration on herself and what she felt. That wing which had always been bent, frozen into a crooked line, had straightened out. It was not wholly as it had been, not as wide-held as the other; still, neither was it crumpled as it had healed in spite of all Simsa's tending.

Zass swam to the edge of the pool, ran forward out of it. Both wings raised, to fan the air, the crippled one almost equalling the other. The zorsal cried aloud, prancing on all four feet at Simsa's side, both wings in motion. It was clear that she was demanding from the girl notice of this healing which had now come to her.

Then it was that Simsa fully remembered! She had not been alone. Nor did she recall ever entering that strange pool, of pulling off her travel worn, sweat-stiffened clothing. Where was he?

On her knees she looked around quickly. The sense of being inside a cup or basin was still very strong. There had been no lightening of the mist. Indeed, to her, it looked even thicker. The silver dust held no tracks—it could not. Move and it straightaway fell into place so that not even the impression of her body was left. A little distance away lay the muddle of her clothing.

Simsa stood, looking slowly around the circumference of the pool. No one else was anywhere within the mist wall. What she could remember last was watching the off-worlder shed his clothing. She glanced quickly in that direction to see if there was that discarded suit. Nothing there. What had happened to her?

He must have stripped her, put her into the pool. She reached her bundle of clothing in a couple of strides, dropped down to explore, there were those two bits of ancient jewelry, the bag of silver which had weighted her sleeve during all their journey.

Her nose wrinkled as she straightened out the breeches, the bits of ragged under-linen, the heavy sleeved jerkin. The touch of them now made her feel dirty, and she felt as if she never wanted to see them again. However all she had carried was still there—a twist of rag with the necklace, another holding the arm guard.

Here in this place of silver and milky-moon radiance Simsa freed the two pieces. The arm guard she slipped over her thin wrist. It was not fashioned for such as she, the thing was too massive, too wide. The necklace with its pale green stones—she brought out a bit of the broken silver, twisted off a thin, stem-like bit to join the open links, then dropped the mended treasure over her head. Cool to the touch, it lay across her shoulders, the green stones fell between her breasts, having been set in a longer bit which nearly touched her waist. She liked the wearing of it. The metal felt right, good. As the ring had done, to wear this gave her the sensation it was meant to be hers.

She retied the bag of silver. He must have seen her treasures when he took her clothing from her. If so, he had left them to her. He . . .

But where *was* he?

The silver necklace slipped smoothly over her body as once more she turned to look carefully about the cup of the pool. All three of the zorsals had once more gone back into the water, were floating there as Zass had been when the girl had first seen her.

Only there was no long, pale body also there, no pile of clothing on the silver of the dust. Nor—had they pulled the carrier into this place? Simsa had a dim memory of that. But it was gone. Her hand clutched, then tightened one about the other so that the tower of the ring caused a small sharp pain. She was alone, and she had not the least idea in what direction she must go to leave, from which direction they had come—where into the mist she dared venture.

That sense of content and well being which had held her when she had awakened, floating in the water, was gone. She stooped and started to dress, though she hated the feel of the grimed and sweat stiff cloth against her body. The zorsals—if they could be persuaded to leave the pool, would they point her a way out? What had led the off-worlder to desert her here?

As she wound the belt about her middle, Simsa clucked enticingly. For a long moment or two she thought that she could not draw them away from the pool. Then Zass, using her crippled wing better than Simsa had ever seen, turned and paddled with all four limbs, the two younger following her.

They came out on the silver dust and trooped to her feet, not taking into the air, rather squatting down to look up at her with those over-large eyes, the darker rings of fur about them seeming to give them a wide and knowing expression.

Simsa waved her hand in the gesture she had trained them to respond to—the one that when sent them out to scout, and uttered the alerting cry.

Obediently the two younger arose, sending the silver

dust fanning out by the motions of their wings. Their antennae uncurled with a snap as they began to fly around the edge of the pool, only they faced always outward, towards the swirling of the mist.

The girl stooped to catch up Zass, and settle her in her old place on the shoulder, taking a queer kind of comfort from the pinch of the large hind feet as they near pierced the coat to her flesh.

Simsa's head was up, she listened intently. So quiet was it here that she could hear the flap of the zorsals' wings in the air. Once she half lifted her hand to her mouth as if to make a trumpet of that, shout through it. She did not quite bring herself to attempt that call.

Rather she also began a circuit of the pond's edge. Some trick of vision made it look smaller than it was in truth, for, as she kept on, still she did not reach the other side of the cup. Then the youngest of the zorsals flashed overhead, straight into the mist uttering a signal, his brother hard on his heels.

Zass's antennae were rod-stiff, pointing in the same direction. Simsa drew a deep breath. Whether she was indeed on the trail of the vanished off-worlder she could not be sure, but the actions of her furred scouts made plain that something of interest lay in that direction.

She was strangely reluctant to leave the pool, the place where she had experienced such a quietude and joy of spirit. At the same time she could not sit here forever. While the fact that the carrier had vanished made her believe that Thom had mean to leave for good. Though why he had abandoned her . . .

The mist wall closed in. She lifted Zass gently from her shoulder, held the zorsal before her so that she could watch the signals of the antennae if they changed direction, which they did—now a few steps to the right, or one or two to the left. For all Simsa knew they might be back circling the pool at another level, still she had no other guide.

Underfoot here was no sand, only rock. Her sandals and the cloth which had bound them to her feet were so badly worn that she could not use them again. So she must go bare of foot and be glad that her soles had been so toughened by years of such usage that, as long as the footing remained damp rock, she could walk it firmly.

Zass's antennae, her whole head, suddenly snapped sharply right. The girl obediently turned in that direction. She believed that the mist was thinner, and, a moment later, was proven right as she came out in a dull grey funnel which fed into a narrower passage. Though she was sure that this was not the way they had come—this ran on a level, no stairs ahead.

The pavement remained smooth, and she was sure not by chance. However, walls were rougher, resembling more the stone of a cavern which had lain in a hill's heart since the beginning of time.

Her journey through the mist had not entirely stripped from her that feeling of well-being she had known after she had been drawn out of the pond. (Why had he done that and yet not waited for her?) She was not afraid—not yet. Rather she was ridden by anger at her desertion—that the off-worlder had walked away and left her—perhaps to death for all he knew.

That anger was mixed with puzzlement. She could understand no reason for such action. Unless, her eyes narrowed a little . . . unless he knew far more about the value of what lay hidden in the Hard Hills and wanted no one to share any such find. Only then, why had he brought her along as far as he had? He could well have deserted her anywhere along the trail and so made *sure* of her death. Why that struggle up the monster-hung cliff? Why had he left her half within what she could only believe was a sort of healing water after her strength had broken at last? Simsa could not fit any of this into a pattern she could understand.

The light which the mist had provided diminished the farther she advanced into the passage. However, there was another gleam ahead, brighter—perhaps that of the day itself. She hurried her pace towards that, suddenly wanting more than anything to be back in an outer world she could understand, even if she faced desert once more, and that alone and without supplies.

What she emerged into was not desert—though the sky held the pitiless sun. Rather she stood in a stone-walled pit—square in shape. In fact it might have been a chamber half hewn from the natural stone. Above her was a crazy patchwork of holes into which might once have been fitted beams to support other floors. The zorsals flew in a back and forth pattern and called to her impatiently.

However she climbed with caution, testing each hand and foothold as she went. There was no stair here; perhaps when the floors existed the lower levels had been entered by trap doors and ladders. This close to the walls, first rock and then dressed stones fitted securely together, Simsa could see the marks of fire. Most had been weathered away, but here and there in protected places there were still black and direful tokens of disaster.

She reached the first large break in that wall, a niche into which she could pull her whole body and from where she could view all that lay immediately ahead. That this had been either a huge fortress, larger than any palace compound of a Guild Lord, or else a small city, there was no doubt.

Its walls had been remarkably well preserved in many places, but here also was greenery. So lush a growth, where she had been expecting to view more barren desert land, that Simsa blinked and blinked again, thinking at first this was some mirage such as she had heard might be sighted by those who traveled too far into the forbidden lands. The greenery did not vanish.

The complex of walls about her were so vine ridden that only here and there a protruding carved stone broke free. Those stones appeared to form a series and each was a head, easily twice the size of her own. Nor were any two of those she could scan from here alike. Some were animals — she was sure that the nearest was a representative of a zorsal, even though the antennae had been broken off quite close to the skull. Others were clearly of her own general species, yet each an individual, as if portraying someone who had lived here once.

Simsa could easily drop from where she perched to the top of another wall, one whose width near rivaled a lane in Kuxortal. Only, at her examination of that, the girl saw the first proof that the zorsals had guided her on the off-worlder's track. There was a pulpy mass of vine where something the length of the carrier might have rested for some time, and beyond that a tree, lacking a branch, its leaves on those above and below scorched and drooping.

It would seem that for some reason this Thom had seen the necessity to move this way, and perhaps swiftly, forcing a path through or against anything which would delay him. Simsa thought she did not need to fear coming on him without an alert—the zorsals would see to that. However, she was determined to follow, if for no other reason than she must know why he had gone.

The path along the top of the wall continued to display a number of traces of hasty passage. As she went, Simsa's winged companions circled back and forth above her head. They were, of course, also by their very attendance, signalling to any who might be watching that she was here.

As she had passed the burnt tree she had paused to examine it. It was well known that the starmen had fearsome weapons. They could blast into nothingness their enemies or their prey. However it was also one of their own laws, which they enforced rigorously, that these potent arms were never carried by any coming to a world such as hers. Only, neither were they supposed to bring any such marvel as the thing that had lightened the carrier. If Thom had broken one law of his own kind, what would keep him from breaking another?

She did not like those signs of burning and edged past that place at a much slower pace. After all, who could judge the ways of an off-worlder? They had customs and codes of behavior far different, such that those of another planet might not even understand. Thom was driven by a great need, or he would not have struck into the desert, would never have come this far.

Another wall arose before her. Here the stepping stone to bring her to its summit was a carved head was a face so horrific Simsa felt a chill. There were the demons and evil things used to frighten children, which one might dream about. As she stared at the thing which now confronted her squarely, she shivered at the pure evil in it.

She found herself making the finger gesture the Burrowers used to evoke fortune (a very fickle presence always in their lives). The worst of this image was not that it wore a grotesque mask of darkness and hate (rather it had a strange beauty which caught and held the eye) but that cruelty, lust, and evil knowledge shone through it in a terrifying way.

To reach the top of the next wall she must mount upon that head. A smear of crushed vine across it proved that he whom she trailed had done just that. Yet she had a feeling that if she drew herself up by its aid she would not feel stone under her feet at all—rather flesh, cold and deathly flesh!

Simsa set her teeth. She must not allow such fancies to disturb her. She was of the Burrowers and had faced much which was of the dark of man's making, knowing it for what it was and refusing to be caught in any trap it devised.

Reaching out she swung up on the head, quickly. As soon as she had secure balance, again seeking hand holds of the edge of the wall above, scrambling up and over that in a haste she could not suppress. The giant face was so real; not the fancy of some perverted artist, rather a true portrait. But if this one had been a ruler here once—then this was a city—or keep—which must have had a fearsome history.

From the roof on which she now crouched, for it was a roof and not another wall top, the girl could look down into a very large court—perhaps even a market square—where vegetation had grown unchecked for a long time. Vines interwove among trees, dead bushes were clasped tightly by their living descendants or by a stranger species which had choked them out. Immediately below her was a strip of bare pavement fully as wide as the wall top.

On this stood the carrier, its cargo still lashed into place—not a single knot untied. Of the off-worlder there was no sign at all.

With a motion of her hand Simsa sent the wheeling zorsals down towards that wilderness. They swooped above it, sometimes venturing to half alight on some top branch, leaning forward, their antennae weaving, always pointing groundward. Like most creatures who depend on flight as one of their defenses, she knew they were reluctant to venture any deeper into that maze of growth. However the senses centered in their antennae must be well aware of any of the forms therein. If the off-worlder had tried to penetrate that choked pit of vegetation they would tell her. For the moment Simsa remained prudently where she was, watching the zorsals carefully, yet dividing her attention between them and what else she could see of this mass of crumbled building, or buildings.

Well beyond the farthest wall (she wished she had the distance glasses the off-worlder carried) she thought she could pick up another mountain looming above this lost place as the cliff had loomed above the desert plane. This might lay on a plateau, or even be part of a valley with the real beginnings of the Hills beyond.

From the zorsals she gained nothing. It became plain there was no value in her remaining where she was. Also, for the first time since she had awakened in the embrace of the pool, Simsa felt hungry. There was still food and water on the carrier, she could see the containers of both, and neither had been loosened. If the off-worlder had intended any long trek from here surely he would have helped himself to supplies.

With caution she descended, using a swing of vine,

already stripped of its leaves, the same way Thom must have reached the ground. As she stood at last by the carrier she could see something which had not been visible from above. The wall at either end of the bare walk on which their crude transport now rested was indented into a doorway, so deep set under an outcrop of a ledge as to be hidden except to one at ground level. While standing within each—

Simsa wheeled, her back against the carrier, her hand going to the hilt of a knife, far too puny a weapon to offer any defense against *that*—or *that!* This was the first time the zorsals had failed her. Why had they not recorded this peril?

She pushed Zass roughly down farther into the front of her jacket, striving to be free to climb to safety as she backed away from the carrier heading for that vine down which she had so foolishly slid.

There was no movement, no advance. The stiffness of those watchers never altered. Their eyes were on her, still there appeared to be no recognition that she was an intruder, the enemy. She halted, glanced to Zass. The zorsal was complaining, yet she never turned its antennae towards either of those *things* in the shadows of each deep doorway.

Her back to the wall, one hand on the vine, Simsa waited. Those two guardians might be chained in place, did they wait for her to come to them? Was that what Thom had done—gone to meet death so?

None of her three furred people so much as looked at them. What defense did these watchers have to deaden the keen senses of the zorsals? The girl gathered Zass closer to her, turned the creature to face that figure at her left.

This was no beast. It stood on two legs, even as she, held a little forward two arms. Still . . .

Zass had at last uncurled her antennae, turned them in the direction of the waiting guardsman, then looked up into Simsa uttering a questioning and slightly guttural sound. No life? Naught but a carved figure?

The girl shifted the zorsal up to her shoulder and walked forward slowly, hesitating every few steps to survey the thing. Under that overhead was dark shadow. Only those eyes which had served her in night running, in Burrow delving, made out features of this silent watcher she could not catch when she had been more dazzled in the light. It was a figure, not of stone—no stone had such a sheen. But if it were metal then why was it so bright, so untouched by time?

Now it became plainer that withered leaves of other seasons, other debris from the growing place, had drifted about to hide the figure's feet, risen up to what might be its knees. Shaped roughly like her own species, yes, but never of flesh and blood.

Simsa walked steadily forward, no longer fearing any attack from its fellow at her back—for that must be twin to this. At length she stood just before it looking up, for it was the taller—perhaps even more so than the off-worlder. The figure *was* of metal of some sort—a dark substance over which there was a patchwork of very faint color following no pattern at all. The head was a huge, round ball, the front of which was a of a different type of material—clear . . .

Having risen on tiptoe to peer through that, Simsa screamed, cowered away. Those dead dried things back on the beach had been noisome enough—but this shriveled, withered thing which stared back at her with eyes which were no longer eyes—it was an abomination she could not bear to look upon!

She turned and ran, back to the carrier, Zass screeching, both other zorsals now fluttering about her head, adding terrified cries to the din their mother made. Simsa tripped and near fell. She clutched the carrier with both hands and clung there, so sick and shaken that she could not even think. Always she had believed that she could face anything—life in the Burrows was never for the squeamish—but this . . . this death of someone locked into metal, left so . . .

Who had stationed those terrible dead as guardians in a broken city? And why? They had been here a long time. Did the power which had put them there still exist? She yet held to the carrier, taking deep breaths, trying to get her emotions under control. The dead could not move, they held no harm in them. She need not—

Then once more she cried out. There *was* movement there; the thing, it was coming for her! She felt as if she were as securely rooted as the tangle of plants behind her, no longer even able to scream, for her throat seemed to close. One of those metals claws hanging by the guardian's side could have thus reached to cut off her breath.

barbe

10.

The zorsals reacted to her fear, wheeling down, darting back and forth right over her head, their screams becoming screeches of rage. Zass fanned her wings frantically, the drooping one rising farther than she had ever been able to use it since her maiming, her head up, deep cries echoing from her. She had come running to Simsa down the carrier, to now face, with the girl, that figure moving out of the deep shadow that held the dead guardian, into the light.

Simsa would have fallen had not the carrier supported her: Thom!

He edged around the stiffly standing dead thing, to emerge into the sunlight. In his hands was a queer rod which Simsa had not seen him carry before. She watched him fearfully. His abandonment of her—were they not enemies because of something she did not yet understand?

Only there was no frown on his face, rather she read concern there. Or was that concern not for her, but rather because she had managed to follow him?

As he came forward, Simsa backed away, edging along the carrier, for at that moment she could not trust her own feet to support her unaided. She was still weak with

175

the panic which had struck her moments earlier.

"It's all right."

She only half heard his words, still backing. Having reached the end of the carrier she kept that between them. Supported as it was, riding higher than it had during the journey through the desert, it bobbed and shifted under her hold.

"It is all right!" he repeated. Now he paused as if she were a frightened zorsal that must be spoken to patiently and slowly until its inner alarm stilled so that one might approach and soothe it by touch as well as voice.

The zorsals themselves were quieting. She had half expected that, motivated by her own fear, they might have flown at him. Instead they now settled beside their dam on the carrier, though they all faced him — their antennae outstretched and quivering.

Somehow Simsa summoned control. This was no nightmare dead thing. Strange as off-world powers might be, Thom was a live creature who could be injured, fight, die; he was not invincible and she knew many tricks. Her retreat stopped, though she stil kept her grasp on the carrier, one part of her mind thinking out a plan to push that forcibly into his path if he tried to rush her.

Though the actions of the zorsals continued to puzzle her. Zass, at least, had for many seasons been a weapon for her mistress, ready to attack upon command. Now it would seem that the older zorsal picked up no hint of trouble from the off-worlder.

Puzzled, thrown off of her usual alert reaction to any hint of danger, her self-confidence badly damaged by what she was now ashamed of — her display of fear — Simsa blurted out the last words she really wanted to speak.

"You left me." Those no sooner had been voiced than she would have given all she possessed to have not broken silence at all.

He still came no closer. That thing he was holding—it must be a weapon. Though it had no blade, no point, nothing about it which Simsa could recognize as a threat. She darted a quick look to her right—could she dodge into that tangle of greenery and so lose him?

"Yes."

His assent again threw her off balance. She had so expected some lie, some explanation, even some sign of shame or need to assure her that what she knew to be true was not. Now she simply stared at him.

She could be as blunt and she had to know. When he added nothing to that she demanded: "Why?"

The off-worlder had not put aside his weapon. Though the zorsals' attitudes would have her judge that he wished her no harm, that he was in no way hostile, yet she had the proof in his very word that he had willingly abandoned her.

"There has been death here." Now he held that weapon in his left hand only, with his right he touched one of those many things hanging from his belt—this a narrow strip of some dark material—which looked like metal such as she had . . . of course, it was like that substance which enclosed the dead guardians!

"There is still death here." She regained much of her self-confidence, now she was able to nod at the frozen figure behind him as if it were no more than a carving of stone.

"That is not what I meant," he returned.

"This," he unhooked the strip of metal from his belt and held it up. Her eyes were keen enough to catch a play of color across it. "This indicates radiation. My people are immune to a high degree. It is part of our history. There was once a war fought on my world, such a war as," Thom looked around him as if he needed some inspiration, something he could draw upon to make things clear to her, "such a war as luckily this planet has never seen. Though it certainly has some surprises of its own to offer.

"There were weapons used which killed—"

She recalled the blasted tree, "By shooting fire? Such a thing maybe as that?" Releasing her grip on the carrier, she pointed to the rod he carried. "I saw—the burnt leaves, the withering."

"This is only a small, a very small example of such weapons." He did not explain, she noted, how he had come by what he held; she was very sure he could not have brought it with him through the desert. The thing was too large to have been concealed anywhere among their belongings.

"No," he was continuing, "there were other fire throwers, such as could consume all of Kuxortal within a flash of thought. Much of my world died so. There were left only small pockets which held life. And the few of my own species who survived—they changed—or their children did. Some died because the changes were such as they became monsters who could not live. A few, so very few, were still human in form. Only they were now born armored against the force of weapons such as those that had killed their world—unless the fire touched them directly.

"For it is also the curse of such a war that the very air was poisoned. Those who breathed it, ventured into certain places, died, not quickly as in the fire, but slowly and with great pain and suffering. Back there—that pool . . ."

"It kills?" she asked slowly. But she had felt no pain. Perhaps that was yet to come. She refused to allow herself to think that she might be akin to those withered, sun-baked things by the shore. Or, worse still, come to be what she had seen in the shell of metal.

"No, I think not." He looked honestly puzzled. "Tell me, how did you feel when you were out of the water—or whatever that liquid may be?"

"Good. And look at Zass." Simsa made up her mind she would not believe that she had been floating in something which would leave her dead. "She can unfold her bad wing; almost, she can fly again."

"Yes. It renews. Only there is something also near here which is the opposite; it kills!"

Now he did begin to move closer to her but this time Simsa did not shrink away. He was holding out that strip of metal he had worn, in open invitation for her to look at it.

"When I came out of the pool—after I had drawn you in, since you were not conscious, nor able to help yourself—I found this thing you see. So I pulled you part-way out and came to explore because of what can be read here."

Thom placed his rod weapon on the pavement, pointed now with his free hand to the strip. There was a distinct line of red upward along it.

"This showed me danger—the very danger which my kind know well from their own past. It might have meant that before us was death—perhaps not for me, but for you and your creatures. I had to find the source, know whether or not there was a deadly radiation."

"You took the carrier," Simsa pointed out.

Again he nodded.

"If there was the degree of radiation which this indicated, then the food, the water on it might already be poisoned for you. I had to make sure that you did not eat or drink before you left the pool chamber and I was not there to warn."

"And *is* what we brought poisoned?" She wondered if he knew that this tale was a weak one. She would have laughed had this been told to her by another, yet she could not judge the off-worlder by the measure of the men in Kuxortal. He was different—and perhaps she was a four-time fool to ever put any trust in him.

"No. The source of the trouble lies there—" He half turned, to point backwards at the Guardian, or perhaps to the passage beyond that motionless figure, from which he had come.

"And where did you get that?" It was Simsa's turn to point—this time to the weapon he had laid down.

"Where I came out into the open. It was just lying there—"

"But not of this city," she prodded when he hesitated. "How did a weapon from the stars—and those—" she indicated the guardian, "arrive here? Did they come then with your brother? Or were they on that ship which you said landed secretly? I thought that it was the rule that you did not bring such weapons to a world where they were not known. These who have waited so long, do they not wear the garments which are also of star ships? I have heard of such—which allow one to walk on those worlds where one cannot breathe the air or live without protection. Who came thus?"

"These have nothing to do with T'seng. They have

been here far longer and our people knew nothing of them. There is a small flyer, not one from the stars, but one such we use to explore new worlds. It rests beyond," he nodded again to the passage, "where it crashed. There was fighting here—a long time ago. Perhaps between outlaws and the Patrol." He stooped to pick up the weapon once again. "There is only a half-charge in this, less now since I tried it. Also this weapon is of a type which is very old and not in use any longer."

He had an answer for everything, Simsa thought, which did not make her feel any easier. That wonderful sensation of well being which had been hers when she had come forth from the pool, that was still a part of her body perhaps, but it no longer soothed and filled her mind. She was retreating fast into the mold of the Burrowers where trust was too high a price for anyone to pay.

"Was this really," she was guessing now but the thought which had come to her suddenly seemed to make sense, "what your brother sought here?"

"Of course not!" Impatience lent a snap into his answer. "But . . ." His oddly shaped eyes changed in a fashion to give him a speculative look, somewhat eager. She could almost see Zass in him now—a Zass who had sensed a ver-rat near to hand. "But perhaps this would explain better why my brother did not return!"

"He was slain by dead men?"

"This!" He seemed not to have heard her retort, instead he held that off-world weapon out at full arm's length, surveyed it as if he had indeed unearthed some treasure which would give him the wealth of a river captain after a full season's fortunate trading. "Tell me, Simsa, what would one of your Guild Lords offer for such weapons, weapons which can kill at a distance, putting their bearers in no danger, but blasting the enemy entirely?"

"You spoke of fire, of cities being eaten up by it," she pointed out. "What good would it do to destroy all that which could be traded for? No lord would send out his guards if he got no loot in return—not even one of the northern pirates would be so foolish. And they will risk more than any trader. The Lords live for trade, not the destruction of it."

"Only, such as this would not level a city. Its range is very limited. At its widest setting it could not destroy more than would be on this carrier."

Simsa looked from the slender rod to the carrier. She had seen the destruction on the upper wall, but what did any Burrower really know of the feuds of the Guild Lords, or the thieves' leaders? Men died in formal duels, in feuds. There had always been raiding of the river convoys, pirates in the northern seas.

Weapons such as this would make a raid harmless for those who used them, and they could take, say, the fleet from Saux, the richest prize ever to set anchor in Kuxortal. It would be as a flock of zorsals lighting upon a pack of ver-rats caught in the open with no holes ready gnawed for their escape.

"You begin to understand? Yes, given ambition, greed, the need for power over others—"

"You think of Lord Arfellen!" She made that a statement not a question. "Men have started talking of him behind their hands. The river trader—Yu-i-pul—last season he brought down such a cargo of weft-silk as most of the city marveled. He would not put it to auction after the custom, but held it, held it in Gathar's warehouse." (The significance of that—maybe it meant something). "Yes—Baslter's story—Baslter's story!"

It was like puzzling out one of the ancient pieces of carving and coming suddenly on a bit which, when fitted into its rightful place, gave meaning to the whole of the find.

"What was Baslter's story?"

Simsa wrinkled her nose. "He is a great zut and would have men afraid of him—always he speaks much of what he knows—so that few listen to him and know that there is ever a grain of truth in his yammering. But he would have it that one of Yu-i-pul's guard got sick-drunk on that rot-wine in the Shorehawl and said that there was trouble, that Yu-i-pul knew an auction would not be profitable because of some meddling, and therefore he would wait out the coming of the ship traders himself. Which he did, though all the city knew that Lord Arfellen was in a rage. It is said that he killed the one who brought him some news of the matter. But the cargo was in Gathar's warehouse in spite of the Guild Lords and Yu-i-ul took home more in trade than any river man has ever hauled upstream. There were five barges and his men were armed with good swords and spears which he had forged for them under his captains' own inspection.

"That was a season ago. Only—what Yu-i-pul has done, so can another river man try. If it goes so, and the auctions are used less and less, then the Guild Lords will feel the pinch."

Matters which had meant nothing to a Burrower, nothing to her save that it had been the initial coming of the very perishable cargo into Gathar's care which had led him to make the bargain with her for the zorsal use (there was a taste or smell to weft-silk which drew ver-rats as sweet gum could draw the Burrow insects).

"Have cargoes coming down the river ever been

plundered?"

"It has been tried many times. Sometimes such did change hands and those bringing the barges into Kuxortal have washed their blades of trader blood well up stream. But the traders of the river road are no weaklings. Such as Yu-i-pul have men sworn to him and his family, father to son. They have stakes in the selling and it is partly their own gain which they would fight for. Yu-i-pul has battled off several attacks in past seasons. They know enough of him and his men now to let his Red and Gold Serpent pennant pass through any of the narrows without challenge. That was why he could say no auction. The Guild wanted no fighting along the wharves, for threaten one river trader in the city and all will answer his warn-war horn, even if they would thrust him through the next day in some feud of their own kind."

"So," the off-worlder dropped down on the pavement, his weapon resting across his knees. He was no longer looking at her but rather at the greenery beyond her shoulder.

Though upper city feuds meant nothing, the more Simsa had talked, the more her own thoughts had leaped from one known fact to a new surmise. As he had done she relaxed, seated herself, giving the carrier a light shove so that it bobbed a little away, no longer any barrier between them.

"You think that if Lord Arfellen knew that such as those," she pointed to the rod, "were to be found here he would send men to seek them out, arm his guard, and venture up river to wait for Yu-i-pul? I think so, too. He is not a man to take lightly to insults and Yu-i-pul made him look small in the eyes of those who knew him best — if Baslter's story was the truth. Also he would be afraid that your brother might discover what lay here. But would he not already have taken these weapons and had them hidden?"

"He could not hide what lies there. Any off-worlder chancing upon it would be required to report it to the Patrol. They would send in their own team, to clean up, to make sure that just that did not happen, that nothing of off-world weaponry would be available to such as Lord Arfellen. I do not know why the first ship landing in these hills did not pick up the radiation reports. Or if they did," he hesitated, "more may be behind this than I first believed."

There had come a change into his face which never seemed open to Simsa's eyes. Now there was a tightness about his lips, once more those lids drooped so she could not see what fire might lie in his eyes. There was something harder, stronger, closed and yet sharper about him, as if some emotion within had given him a new and keener purpose.

"You believe your brother is dead?" she asked quietly.

Still he did not look at her.

"Of that I am going to make sure."

That was no oath sworn by blood drip or brother drink, still his words would hold him, of that she was certain. Watching him now she knew that she would not want to be one to whom he threw a feud challenge.

"You think that they have been here—and Lord Arfellen might have sent them. But how would they know anything about it?" Simsa was suddenly struck by that.

If a crashed star ship, or even part of such a one, had been found, that story could never have been suppressed in Kuxortal. There was too much interest always in the spacers and all which pertained to them.

"They might not have known about this—at first. But there have long been stories of treasures hidden in the Hard Hills. So when my brother, an off-worlder, came to hunt for such, might they not have believed that he was in search of something more than the source of very old things?"

Simsa's Burrower shrewdness accepted that. Naturally an off-worlder who came to search the Hard Hills would be assumed by Guild men to be hunting more than broken bits of stone, no matter what might be lettered on such. Though she herself had a lanquid interest in that direction because of Ferwar's addiction and the fact that there was a market among starmen for pieces, she would never have thought that anyone would cross space and then the desert land in quest of those alone, unless he was a victim of some madness.

There was the ring on her hand. She made a fist now by curling her fingers together so that the tower with the gem roof stood stolid and tall. There were those other pieces—the necklace which still rested its pale stones, like the tears shed by a weeping tree, between her breasts, the cuff—

She felt now within her sleeve pocket and brought that out. In the sun here it came to life, not brilliantly, but with a steady glow. At the same time she jerked open the coat to show the gems resting against her dark skin.

"There may be treasure here also." Deliberately she tossed the cuff through the air and saw him, in swift reflective action, catch it.

"These were the best of Ferwar's things. I do not believe that they came originally from Kuxortal. There is nothing about them which is of the city. Nor are the stones as are set here," she picked up the long, narrow strip which formed the pendant and held that into the sun in turn, "any such as I have seen brought overseas or down river.

"The Old One had dealings with faceless ones who made sure that they were not seen coming or going. I do not know from where these came. But it is true that seasons ago there was some small trade with the desert men. Then those came no more and instead there was a story of a plague which killed quickly—"

Though he turned the cuff about in his hands, his attention was no longer for that. Instead he leaned forward, staring at her, his eyes wide open as they seldom were, eagerness visible in every line of his taut body.

"A plague which killed quickly!" he repeated. "Of what nature?"

Again her thoughts took one of those sudden leaps. It was as if her whole mind could half sense what lay in his from time to time. She dropped the pendant back against her breast, waved her ringless hand towards that grim guardian which she could see the best.

"What you said of the air which could carry some poison in it where your weapons had been used— A plague!"

"Yes!" he was on his feet again in one fluid movement. Then turned to demand of her:

"This plague—how long ago?"

The Burrowers did not reckon time, they had no reason to. One season followed another. One said that this or that happened in the year the river rose and Hamel and his woman were drowned, or in the season that the Thieves took Roso to be a climbing man—that was the way the Burrowers remembered. If the Guilds numbered their years Simsa had no way of telling by their time. But she tried to think back to the last time that bone-lean man who had brought Ferwar the most and best of her private gleanings had come to them.

He was a river trader of the smallest fringe of that order, one who could never reckon more profit than might feed him and his crew of two boys, as hungry and meager as himself, for more than a voyage—if they were that lucky. She began to count on her fingers.

"Twelve seasons ago—Thrag came. He had found a desert man by the river, dying. He waited for his death and then took what he had. But," she frowned, "the Old One said it was cursed. She paid him, but said to bring no more and she wrapped it many times over and had me bury it under stones. It was a jar of some kind. I remember she asked Thrag what the desert man died of, and then she was angry and told him that it was a devil and had doubtless touched him also. He ran. Nor—it is true—did he ever come again."

One did not question the Old One, Simsa had learned that as the first and foremost rule of her life, so early she could not remember when she did not know it. Now thinking on what had happened: Thrag, the dead man from the desert, the fact that men had commented that the desert people in the following seasons had disappeared, all came together in another of those quick forming patterns.

"Twelve seasons ago, six of your years," Thom was speaking his thoughts aloud again. "These desert people could have stumbled on a radioactive wreck, plundered it . . ."

"The plague being that kind which slaughtered your people in the long ago? But there was no war here."

"No war for your people that is true. But two enemies,

two ships, one hunting the other, so driven by fear or need for revenge as to loose the last weapon—a crash; it fits! By the Sages of the Ninth Circle, it fits!"

"But you said that what you found was not a ship out of space," she reminded him.

"No. But it could have come from such a ship, used for escape by survivors who were still hunted men."

"And who now stand there—and there!" Deliberately she pointed first to one of those guardians and then to the other. "But why do they stand so? I thought them guards. If they had died of plague or fought and killed each other, then why do they still stand so, one at either end of this way? That is the fashion in which guards of the Guild stand before a door which none but a high one can enter."

Thom turned his head slowly, surveying first one and then the other of the motionless, suited bodies.

"You are right," he said thoughtfully. "There is something very purposeful in the way they were left, perhaps as guards—perhaps for some other reason."

"Were they—" Remembering what she had seen within the bubble-like helmet, she gave a small gulp, and then continued with what easiness she could summon, "Were these of your people? Or could you tell?"

"Not my kind," Thom answered her decisively. "They were warriors. After the ruin which came to my world our way of life was changed. We followed another path and that does not lead to war. If we kill—" She saw him shiver then and under her gaze it was as if his face grew gaunt and older in an instant—"if we take life knowingly and willingly, except to save ourselves or another, then there is that in us which takes command of our minds and we die. We are no longer men!"

She could not be sure of what he meant, but she knew that it was dire. Also she believed that he should not be allowed to think on what her words had summoned to his mind.

"Not your people, then. But you know other worlds. Can you tell from which these came?"

"I shall find out!" He reached forward and dropped the rod on the carrier. She saw the roosting zorsals edge away from it, as if they sensed that it was a thing of dark power. "Indeed, I am going to find out!"

11.

"So," Simsa also arose, "in which direction do we now search? The zorsals can find living things. Dead men wrapped in dead metal they will not hurt."

The two winged hunters were up once more from the carrier, coasting out over the thick stand of green stuff. Simsa could guess that they were hungry and went to prey upon what their acute sensors could pick up, even though day was upon them. Perhaps, because of that stand of thick green, the heat and glare were not so intense here. Or their interlude in the strange pool had heartened them, as she was sure it had done her, to the point that they could bear far more of the day's light.

"We?" then Thom began and she already guessed that he was about to deny her any part in this. However, Simsa had no intention of either remaining here, overwatched by alien dead, or staying purposeless wherever the off-worlder would elect as a place of safety while he ranged outward.

"We!" Simsa repeated firmly. "You say you have found a broken ship. Even if it was not made for star travel, still it was not of this world. If it rode in the air, then how may it be traced to its home port any more than a sea ship can be followed through trackless waves?"

193

barbi

When he did not answer her, she felt a small glow of triumph. Let this off-worlder not believe that he was the only one who could reason with good logic and to the point.

"It would seem that the way these were left," once more she indicated the encased dead, "has meaning. They are not as old as this place—that must surely be true. I think this was long forgotten before they came from the sky. It is—" For the first time she pushed the dead aliens to the back of her mind, thought of those faces she had seen so boldly carved along the walls, especially that special one which had so impressed her, leaving her feeling both frightened, and, in a manner, unclean.

"This is," she continued after a moment's hesitation, "a place of *this* world. And the pool . . ." Hardly aware of what she was doing, she fingered the ring on her hand, rubbing across the stone which had held so much color of that "water" in it. "My people—we of the Burrows—swear by no gods or forces save Fortune. For it is true, I think, that there are none such who concern themselves with us and our fate. Still, in that pool there is life." She spoke as if something else fed the words into her mind. Yet, even as she mouthed them, Simsa was aware also that there was truth in what she said. "I do not know who they were, these people of the Hard Hills. However, it is plain they had secrets of their own, as powerful for us as the flame death is for those of your blood. How felt you when you came from that place?"

"There is some form of radiation there," again he was using a term out of his own knowledge. "Only it is such as I cannot measure. As to how I felt, I was . . . renewed, I think." He had been holding the cuff in one hand, as if it were of little or no importance. Now she saw him suddenly slip it up over his fingers and palm, squeezing those together to allow it to pass. Even as he did that he stood staring down at the band of metal which rucked up a little of the sleeve of his off-world garment.

"Why did I do that?" He seemed as bewildered as if he had been in the power of another, sent a task he did not understand in the least. "It somehow it feels right, but—" He stretched out the same hand for the stock of the rod weapon, jerked back with a cry of mingled pain and shock.

"I—it forbids me to take up that! But this is insane! The sun—I must have had a touch of sun to . . ."

Simsa smiled. So the wonders one could summon here were not so one-sided after all. She herself could supply something which would astound and dismay even one who talked of the destruction of worlds, and of wars flung wide enough to engulf whole legions of stars.

"Perhaps there are also weapons which *your* people do not understand." She pulled at the necklace on her breast, twirled the ring out into the full of the sun. "You hunt one mystery here, starman, there may be others."

He still stared down at the cuff, though he had ceased to try to rid himself of it. Nor did he attempt again to take up that weapon of his own kind. Simsa reached out her arm so that Zass could climb this bridge to the zorsal's usual riding place on her shoulder. A wind had been rising, sending branches and leaves rustling. Even though these grew so closely together her one could not see how even the fingers of a light breeze could reach within the shadows to trouble them. The girl glanced at the sky. To the north clouds massed, a sight she had never expected to see over desert lands, or even this early in the season. Though this growing dark was no surprise to any who knew the way of the wet-time.

She turned to face the guardian in the other section of that way.

"There is rain there." She pointed to the clouds. "Though a storm at this season is unusual, still I guess it best for us to seek cover. You speak of danger lingering in your broken sky-traveling thing, so perhaps it is best we take this other way."

A sudden heavy gust of air swooped down upon them, bringing with it the zorsals, screaming with rage, and, she was sure, a beginning of fear. The creatures caught at the lashing on the carrier and held fast, their teeth fully displayed as they made apparent what they thought of such a freak storm.

The girl stooped and caught at the pull rope of the carrier. For the first time she exerted her strength against the pull of that and felt the thing answer. Perhaps because she still held to that supply of new strength she had brought from the pool she took pleasure in the fact that she was taking the lead in their journey.

Only Thom reached her in two strides, caught the rope out of her hand. He had awakened out of whatever dazzlement or deep thought had entrapped him by the cuff. Now he moved with his old authority and confidence.

A second gust of air bore up sand grit to sting their faces and eyes, actually carrying with it bits of twig and torn leaf. It was as if something about this open space in the long dead keep or city attracted the gathering strength of the storm. Simsa, remembering traders' tales of certain rocks, peaks, even outcroppings of sea reefs, which did pull the fury of tempests, was eager to get under cover.

Their way was still blocked by the suited dead. The space on either side of that standing figure was too narrow for the carrier. Thom did not wait to study the problem. Thrusting the lead rope of the carrier back into the girl's hands, he strode forward to grasp the shoulders of the figure. Though, Simsa was pleased to note, he did not stare at what lay behind the open part of that bubble helmet, rather kept his gaze turned to one side as he exerted strength (and it clearly needed full strength on his part; his muscles stood out visibly under the smooth fitting of his suit) to shove it to one side.

Some inequality of the pavement, or incautious movement on his part had a sudden answer. The dead thing tottered. Simsa cried out, her voice rising above the howling of the zorsals, as it rocked forward. Thom stepped aside just as it crashed, to lie on the pavement, still as stiff and stark in its new position as it had been when it had denied them entrance to the way beyond.

Simsa sidled well away from it as she came on, giving a vigorous jerk to the carrier. Thom stood above the fallen figure with clenched hands, looking down at its back almost as if he expected to see those stiffly suited arms go out, the legs move, and the dead arise to give battle.

The bottom of the carrier rasped across the bubble head of the fallen to nudge against the off-worlder. He gave a start, then stepped wide across it almost as if he feared the dead could reach out, catch at one of his scuffed boots. Then they were both beyond, passing out of the fast fading light of the day where the storm clouds swung slow, into a corridor.

Though this passage grew increasingly dusky Thom made no move toward lighting the lamp at his belt, and Simsa did not want to break the silence of this place by asking for that aid. For, even as they went by the guardian, the zorsals had abruptly ceased to cry.

Under her feet was the velvety gathering of long years of dust, as soft as the silvery sands which had encircled the pool. She glanced down at it now and again but they were already too far advanced into the twilight of the windowless and lightless passage for her to see if that was track-imprinted by any who might have passed this way before.

Outside, the storm hit at last with a roar, which followed them along the corridor like the outraged cry of a hunting beast through whose paws they had luckily escaped. There were flashes, too—lightning had been unleashed.

Still Thom walked, beside her now, his hand on the tow rope not far from hers, allowing the girl to share his responsibility. Zass hissed into Simsa's ear after each lightning flash, flattening her body as close to the girl's shoulder as she could.

The passage was not altogether dark for the further they withdrew from the entrance of the guardian, the more visible came another gleam of light ahead. Twice, warned, or alarmed, by lightning which had given her a momentary glimpse of something leaning outwards from the wall, first on one side and then the other, Simsa had pulled aside. Only to realize that what she avoided were images nearly life size which began to mark the walls at regular intervals. Her first thought was that these were more of the dead.

Perhaps Thom had been startled out of his preoccupation by the same thought. For at last he snapped on his lamp for a fraction of time, only to reveal the figures were of stone not metal. That flash of clear sight had given

Simsa only a swift impression of something man-like, but she wanted to see no more of such.

Instead she centered her gaze steadily ahead to that wan promise of more light. Doubtless the off-worlder had some good reason for his now-cautious use of the lamp. Perhaps its power only lasted so long—even as he had warned her that of the box which lifted the carrier must be renewed.

They emerged at length into grey light again, though they were not fully in the open. Even as they stepped free of the passage Thom cried out, threw hs arm about Simsa to hold her against him, pushing back into the archway behind. Down into the center part of the open space before them smashed a great block of stone, striking with force enough to crunch and send splinters flying in all directions.

Simsa stared up. They were under a roof in which there was a great jaggered crack, through which showed the night dark of the storm. She could see through this gloom other pieces of the dome which had fallen in the past. Thom pulled her to the left, leading her under what seemed a much more secure overhang. Here she was as ready to hug the wall as he was to press her closer to it.

This space was no rough underground cavern. They were separated from the central cathedral and dangerous part by a series of pillars placed in regular order at the edge of the overhang. Each of these was carved in the form of either a standing figure, or a thick stemmed growth, half vine, half tree. All loomed well above even the off-worlder's head. Simsa felt a beginning of curiosity, a desire to inspect them more closely, but her companion did not linger, and urged her on by the grip he still held on her arm.

There were no more openings nor doors in the wall which formed the left side of this covered way. On that space were deep carvings, but no faces leered at her, rather these ran in lines as might some gigantic record left to puzzle those with whom the builders shared no blood tie nor memory.

She could not guess how far they had gone in their half trot along that wall when suddenly there was a flare of light directly ahead—darting upward, then spreading out to catch them both in its beam. There had been no more crashes of stone from above, yet the sound of the storm echoed hollowly here. Thus Simsa caught only a faint sound from her companion.

He dropped his hold on both her and the carrier, whirled, to catch up that weapon rod awkwardly in his cuffless left hand. A leap carried him before her with one end of the rod clapped tightly to his side by his bent arm, his fingers hooked about a projection a third of the way down its length.

That flare ahead did not fade or fail, remaining near as bright as the sun. Simsa had involuntarily shaded her eyes at first, now as her sight adjusted, she first peered between her fingers, and then dropped her hand entirely.

This was not a fire, rather it burned steadily, as might a lamp. A camp? Of whom? No guild force or traders she knew of had such day-clear illumination to serve them.

Then—could the dead have left this on guard for some lost reason?

The girl, recalling only too well Thom's tales of a slaying fire, reached out to sweep the other two zorsals to her. They had hunched their heads between their shoulders, half raised their wings as shields against the glare. She caught their honks of fear and misery. With

Zass still in her usual place on one shoulder, the other two now crowded onto her arm (so heavy a weight together that she had to steady them against her body) Simsa backed against the wall, wondering if she dared to turn and run, believing she was too well revealed to try. She had no doubt that any weapons off-worlders might carry would have a range of least as far as a bow and she was well within arrow length of the light's source.

Thom stood, his feet slightly apart, facing that beacon directly. Now he called out, waited, and called again—three times in all. His voice sounded differently. Simsa half guessed that he was speaking other tongues.

There came no answer save the continued flare of the light. From here she could not even see the source from which that sprung. Thom raised his other hand so she caught the shine of the cuff, waved her to stay where she was. Then he began to walk steadily, with obvious purpose, toward the glare.

Simsa's breath came raggedly as if she had run some race. She waited for fire, for some other strange and horrible fate, to cut him down. There was no belief in her that there could be any friends here.

But no war arrows, cut to whistle alarmingly as they took the air, no spouting of off-world fire, followed. Thom was merely walking as if back in the desert and that light was the cruel heat of the sun.

She could see him so clearly, though only his back now. Still he waited for death to claim him. Then he turned a little from the column of the light, passed to one side to hide—consumed?

The zorsals still cried and clung to her, showing no desire to take flight. Was it the light which kept them so? Or did they sense some greater danger? Their antennae were all closely rolled to their small skulls, and their big eyes squeezed shut.

Then, a dark blot which could only be Thom—she was sure it was—showed once more between her and that light. While the light itself was reduced in both length of beam and harshness of glare, so she could see he stood there waving her forward. Because she must trust him, if she trusted anyone beyond herself in this place, the girl picked up the rope of the carrier, set herself to the forward pull of its weight and obeyed his signal.

By the time she had reached the source of the light it had been softened to hardly more than that which a fire might give on a chill night of the wet-season's ending. Now she could see a space in which there had been set up what seemed to be a kind of fortified camp—if all those lumps of stone had been dragged there for walls of protection.

Piled against these blocks were containers and boxes—some of the type which she had seen unloaded many times from traders' rafts on the river. The others were of metal—surely off-world.

While the light itself came from a cylinder placed on a plate of metal in the middle of the camp. Simsa looked hurriedly around. Where were those who had set the light? She half expected to see, marching towards her, suited bodies—living bodies—of off-worlders. Dead men, she told herself firmly, do not make camps—they do not!

Only there was no one there save Thom. He, however, had no longer any attention for her. Instead he was on his knees by one of the off-world containers, this one thin in width and slightly curved. Simsa thought it might just have been shaped to fit upon a man's back, for straps dangled down the inner side. Thom had flung up the lid of that and was delving inside. Two small boxes, neither much larger than his own hand, had been set out. Then there was a larger one which flapped open as he pulled it free. Inside were blocks which fell out—one bouncing across to Simsa.

She had set the zorsals on one of the barricade rocks, now she stooped to pick up that wandering square—and froze before her fingers quite touched it. She jerked her hand back, old half forgotten stories shifted into her mind.

Caught—a man's, a woman's innermost spirit caught—fastened, made so a possession of another that such a thing could be used to summon, to torment, to—kill! Ferwar had laughed at such tales. But Ferwar—not even the Old One had seen such as this. For what she looked upon must indeed be the root of such stories. She was looking down—at herself. Imprisoned in the transparent cube was a figure so much alive that Simsa could not look aside.

That was how she must have appeared when she had drawn herself up on the silver sand of the pool, before she had pulled on again that dirty and confining clothing. The black skin of the prisoner was rounded, or spare—just as she was so shaped. If she could put finger within that transparent cover surely she would touch flesh. That silver hair curled, as if just tossed in a loosening rain-wind. The ends lay soft across the shoulders, one strand half concealing a small, proud jutting breast. There was no coarse clothing, rather around the trim hips rested a chain as silver bright as the hair. From this hung a kilt fringe of gems strung in patterns made by the use of silver balls between stones—just such gems as those of the necklace.

The small head was proud-high. There was that about this other Simsa—in the block—so great a pride. The living girl drew a deep breath. Through the hair on that high-held head was threaded another chain of gems, so that on the forehead rested a circle of them, pale and green, centered by another stone, opaque, the twin to the ring's jewel.

One of the image's hands held a small rod, appearing to have been wrought from some huge single white-grey gem. It was topped by a symbol Simsa had seen—one repeated several times over in some fragments the Old One had pored over, two curved horns turned upward, supporting between them a ball.

This was she. Yet never had she worn such gems, stood so tall, so unafraid, triumphantly proud! Was this that other her which some said dwelt within the body and went forth—no one could guess where—when life was spilled out forever? How could that be? She was alive here—Simsa as she had always been, had known herself, and yet—there was this other who was also her!

Though she did not realize it, she had knelt, was leaning forward now, one hand planted palm flat on either side of that amazing thing, staring at it, still in shock.

The girl was not even aware the off-worlder had come until his shadow fell across the other Simsa, half veiling her. She had raised her hand to brush that away. Then she looked up, met his eyes. For a moment they rested on her—then on the other one.

He stared so long at the prisoner in the block that she began to feel cold. He knew—without her asking. Without answering, she also understood that he knew the truth of this thing, of what it might mean—and what it might do. She wanted so much to catch up that block, hide it away from his eyes, hiding this other self from his knowing— But it was too late for that.

Now he knelt, too, but he made no effort to take it from her. Could it be that there was a chance that he would let her keep it—make sure that she alone held safe this other self?

"It is—me—me!" She could no longer hold back the words. "Why is it me?"

She raised her eyes, hardly daring to look away from her find, lest he did take it. He had the strength to make it his, past all her defenses, even if she called upon the zorsals. Also he knew what it was and how . . . .

Simsa could not read his expression. She had seen him surprised, she had seen him angry, she had seen him push himself to the edge of endurance. This was another Thom—one she must now fear?

"This—" he spoke very slowly and softly, almost as if he did not want to frighten her. "This is a visa-picture. It was made by my brother."

"Picture." she repeated. His brother—where? She looked around wildly.

"Like the bits on the walls, the heads," he continued just as slowly and carefully. "Somewhere my brother saw this—and copied it so."

"Me!" she insisted.

Thom shook his head. "Not you, no. But plainly someone of your race, your own people, someone whose blood line might still have had a part in your own making. See—I would say she is a little older . . . and look there, do you have such on your body?" He did not touch the block which held the other Simsa, simply pointed with finger tip to the smooth skin just a little above that fringe of gems which fell between the slim, long legs.

Simsa stared. Yes, there was something there—a scar, hardly showing, except that it must stand out in a ridge above the rest of the skin. It was the same symbol as crowned the rod this strange Simsa carried—two horns guarding a ball.

"That—" he told her now, "is X-Arth indeed. Though this woman who wears it—wore it—is of no Arth race I have seen accounts of. Perhaps she was Forerunner—one of those who vanished from all worlds and space before our own kind came into being. That is a very old sign even on Arth, for it combines two forces, the sun and the moon."

"You say she is gone!" Simsa caught him up quickly. "But I am here. If she is not me, then she is kin, as you have admitted. Your brother—he can tell me—we can find—!"

The words poured out, she had not realized that she had reached forward and caught him by both shoulders, was even trying to shake him as if so she could better batter into him her need.

Now the expression on his face was changed indeed. It was not one of that strange softness which he had shown before, rather his features again set, his eyes narrowed and shut against her.

"My brother is—" for a long moment his lips did not move. Then he twisted free from her hold and stood up. "I can only believe that he is dead."

She stared up at him gape-mouthed. Then the full force of what he meant made her snatch at what he called a visa-picture, which she knew she must have. Almost in the same instant she scrambled back against one of the rocks which made up that pocket of the camp. With that stone at her back firm, so comforting, she looked around again.

"How do you know?"

He nodded to the container he had been unpacking. "He would not have left that here, as he did the pilot—" Now he gestured to the lamp which still gave a day's light to them. "Those are intended as guides. They are—it is difficult to explain to one who does not understand our ways—but they are used in times of trouble to bring help. In them is an element which is set to answer to another whom those who may help always carry." Once more he fingered one of those things on his belt of so many wonders. "When I came within the right distance—that blazed—to draw me. Just as it would have drawn any one of our service who came here. Had it not been for the fury of the storm we might even have heard a call, for they are set also to broadcast sound as well as light."

"My brother would have had no reason to set this pilot light unless he believed he was in grave danger. Nor would he have left what he did in that," he pointed to the container, "unless he hoped that it would be found by someone searching for him."

"A message—" she had assimilated what he meant, "did he tell you somehow then what that danger was?"

"He may have." Now he went back and picked up one of the smaller boxes which he had taken from the container. "If he did the message is taped here."

"But this—" she still had the block, holding it with great care. "Would he tell you where this came from? You talk of Arth, X-Arth—of Forerunners—of wild things no one has heard of—you know so much, you of the stars—tell me what you can of this one who looks like me! Tell me!" Her voice arose, she cried out with all the longing of those years in which she had been so much a stranger that she must hide her strangeness from her world. In a mixture of races she had been the most notable that she knew. She remembered only too well again how Ferwar had cautioned her from her earliest childhood to conceal what she could of her strangeness. How many times had the Old One warned of the Guild Lords who might have taken her just for her difference? She accepted the danger and had always done as the Old One said. She had been so long childish of body, she was near twice as many seasons as the rest of the Burrower girls when they were sought to pleasure some man. Partly she had been safe because she so long remained a scrawny child. It was only when she had come out of that pool really that she had known pride in her body as well as in her wits.

"If I can find where that—where he saw it—" Thom said, slowly, "then I shall take you there. If we come forth from this venture still alive."

She looked down at the Simsa in the block. He was right—she might want passionately to find this, but perhaps death stood in their way. Still, this much she had and it gave her a fierce joy of possession as she looked upon it.

12.

Though the storm still rolled overhead, and there had been at least one more crashing fall of stone in the outer part of this great chamber, Simsa sat at ease. In one hand she held a small container which Thom had given her, after showing her how to twist the upper part a little and then wait for a short time so that when it was fully opened what it held was hot as if just poured from some inn kettle. She savored the rich contents, picking out bits which she handed down to the eagerly reaching paws of the zorsals, the three gathered before her and watching each bite she transferred to her mouth. Off-world food, with a savor she had never dreamed that any food could have.

Thom had another such can by this knee where he, too, sat cross-legged. Only his attention was not for the food, but rather for the sounds made by the small box he had told her might contain any message his brother might have left. The sounds were not speech as Simsa recognized as such, rather a series of clicks as one might rap out with a bit of metal against stone. At her comment, before he had waved her impatiently to be still, Thom said that this was a secret way of message sending and only one trained could make sense of those clicks.

211

The girl yawned as she scooped out the last large piece of food, then put the can down so that the zorsals squabbled over the chance to lick out its interior with their long tongues. She would have liked to have explored, poked into the remaining boxes and containers. On the other hand she also felt drowsy, and, for the first time since she had left the pool, at ease and content. That the camp had not been looted, Thom had said, meant that his brother had not been either killed or taken captive here. Thus he appeared to believe that they were safe also—at least for now.

Simsa stretched out, turned her head a little so she could watch those lines of patterns across the wall. Among them she searched for that symbol connected with the other Simsa. Only it appeared nowhere here, at least not within the range of her sight. Then the clicking came to a sudden stop, and she looked toward the offworlder.

He had picked up the box with the message, was sitting with that closed-face look which she knew meant he was thinking.

"What did it tell you?" This silence had stretched too long—she wanted to know. Perhaps within those clicks was even the secret of what meant the most to her.

"He discovered that he had been followed. He had made a find—Arth—Forerunner— Then he saw the ship. There was enough about it—though he did not give details—to make him afraid that it might be the wreck of a war spacer. It was hot—radioactive—but he thought not too high for one of our blood to explore. He scouted and found indications that there had been others before him. Some of them, at least, were desert people; he discovered at least two bodies of those."

"Only," the off-worlder sat back on his heels, interlacing his fingers and turning them in and out, his eyes upon their movement as if so he worked some kind of fortune producing ritual, "he also came across signs that there had been another landing by several smaller ships—and not long ago. There had been a camp near there. A meeting place for those of this world . . . and others. Jacks!" The last word came as an explosion.

"Who or what are Jacks?" she pulled herself up. To learn all that from a series of clicks! But this was another starman's thing and so it could be true.

"Outlaws," he returned. "Just as you have pirates on your seas, so do we have their like along the star lanes. Such could provide the means for looting that war spacer. They would do so if the price was high enough. They have been and gone, but they had also left a beacon, something such as that—" he gestured to the lamp, "but of a different kind, in that it can be heard off-world by the ship for which it is set. When they left the beacon it meant they planned to return. It could be that they did not have equipment enough to start scavenging, or it might be that they needed more help, or—" He waved his hand as if there could be ten-ten reasons for such a visit and a promised return.

"They might want what they found for themselves; then the Guilds have nothing to do with this."

Thom shook his head. "That camp my brother found remains of was laid out first by men of this world—the others were visitors. Also it was set up several season ago, and therefore whoever dealt with the Jacks knew well enough what lay here. Only that they themselves could not yet make use of it."

"If they knew, say, Lord Arfellen . . ." Simsa began

once more to fit piece to piece in her mind. "Then why did they let your brother come here? He was off-world, he would know at once that this wreck of a ship was a bad thing. They could have easily killed him before he reached the Hills at all—"

"Unless they dared not report a death near their own territory—even by accident—of an off-worlder. My brother was no common man and the League and the Patrol keep their watch on all of us, especially when we come to hunt out Forerunner remains—or things X-Arth. Can you understand, Simsa? It is not the actual worth of bits of broken stone, or this," he tapped the cuff he still wore, "which matter. We seek out all we can learn because we must!

"My people spread out from Arth itself so many seasons ago that you would have difficulty in counting time. We found worlds with others living there—some were strange of body, stranger yet of mind. Some were enough like ourselves that we could interbreed. Other worlds were empty of life, yet held broken cities, strange machines, mysteries left by intelligent beings.

"All we can learn we must, for there were many, many powers which rose among the stars—and then fell. Some fell by war—we have discovered worlds which have been burnt black, holding only ashes—the result of the use of such weapons as we have come to fear and have outlawed. But also there were other worlds where all that remained appeared as if those who dwelt there had simply walked away and left great wonders to be toppled by the fingers of time.

"Why did they rise to power and fall? If we can learn only a little of their past then we can foresee the way of our own future, at least in part. Perhaps some of the acts which brought them down we can then avoid."

"There is one world in our League where all such finds are gathered to be studied. The race who live there—who are so long-lived a species that to them our oldest known are but infants—study these finds, try to learn. Sometimes they themselves are the searchers, more often it is we of other species and races who collect the knowledge for them. Such a searcher was my brother—and he had much experience in these matters. When the first star ships landing here brought back fragments of a much older time, and our traders brought ever more, he was chosen to come and see—to make records—report whether the remains here were such as would warrant sending in a whole ship of trained people to deal with them."

"My Simsa"—she still thought of the picture as that—"was she of your Forerunners? These people who rose and then fell, who knew once the stars and then lost them?"

"Perhaps—those symbols make it seem likely. Or she could be one born of this world who learned of such from other star rovers—those who were star rovers before my people lifted from their own world at all. I know now where T'seng found her."

"Where? Let us go there!"

"If you wish—" he sounded almost indifferent. He was more intent, she must accept, on his own search, the plans he must make. "In the morning," he added.

Simsa knew she must be content with that. Though she longed to set out at once, he had risen, gone to the lamp. Now he passed across it a disc he had taken from his belt. The light winked out. As its going the zorsals stirred and the girl gave the signal which would post them as sentries.

She was sure that she could not sleep—that the need to see that other Simsa was so aching, tearing a feeling that she could not rest. But sleep lay in wait for her after all.

She awoke to the sound of water. Grey light from beyond the rock walls of the camp site, shined through the broken dome so far overhead with the brightness of at least an hour past dawn. Across the camp's space Thom lay, the arm with the cuff covering his eyes as if he had gone to sleep trying to shut out some sight he must rid himself of—at least for a while.

Simsa heard a soft chitter. The three zorsals were roosting on the top of one of the rocks, their softer, sleepy voices signifying they were settling for sleep. She got to her knees and looked out into the center of this space which was larger than any building in all of Kuxortal.

Now, in the better light, she could see that it was oval in form and that ranked above this covered, arched way which appeared to run completely around the oval, were tiers of ledges, as if those had once furnished seats or resting places. People must have gathered here for some purpose. Probably to view action in the center where those lumps of broken masonry had crashed to crumble. She had never seen such a place and she wondered what could possibly bring so many people together—if all those ledges had once been filled.

The water she had heard running—that was funneled off from the ledges and the broken dome, gathering in a channel not too far from the camp. Simsa crawled over the rock barrier and went to it. It seemed clear and drinkable. She palmed up some, went back to offer it to Zass, who obligingly lapped her tongue twice across the girl's palm, thus declaring it all right. All that talk of plague from Thom's "radiation" warning made Simsa doubly cautious, but now she drank and found it good.

"Fair morning to you, Lady Simsa—"

She had been trying to comb her tangled hair with her fingers, now she looked over her shoulder and smiled. Her waking here had seemed so lacking in care, as if they were safe in spite of all Thom's tales. She found herself light of heart again, as she had been when she had left the pool.

There was something else she noted with a small inner surprise. When he had called her "Lady" before she had believed he had jeered at her, making it plain she was of the Burrowers, but—now—that title seemed right.

"It is a fair morning, Lord Thom—" she agreed. "If you will toss me that water container I can fill it before last night's bounty runs dry."

Already the run-off water stream was diminishing in size.

He did just as she had suggested, she using her lightning skill to snatch it out of the air, catching at its cording so it swung around her arm. This easily carried piece of equipment also had been among their finds the night before, and Simsa had guessed that its being left there was one more reason her companion believed in his brother's death.

She filled, rinsed, and filled it again. If they were to go on (she had already marshalled facts and plans) they could not burden themselves with the unwieldy and hard to handle carrier. Instead they must draw upon the camp equipment. It would appear that was just what Thom was prepared to do. Those things which had been in the one pack he had opened and explored so fully, he laid into a hamper, filling the first with ration tins and other things he sought from here and there among all which had been stored in the camp.

That light-weight, very tough, and yet silken smooth square which had served as a folded pillow for Simsa was trussed to form a second pack which Thom fussed over until he was sure that it would ride easily on her back. As he worked he explained the use of some of the things they must carry. There were direction finders which would pick up those trail markings T'seng had set up leading Thom along his brother's explored paths. In addition were some small, round balls Thom explained were to be pressed at one end and then tossed. Almost instantly thereafter they loosed clouds of mist that would over-power any animal or unprotected humanoid creature. There were only four of these, but Thom divided them, insisting that Simsa carry her pair in sleeve pockets she could easily reach.

She had already turned out of her right one the bag of silver bits—useless here, weighing her down when she could well need an extra lightness of arm.

When the packs were both put together, Thom picked up the case into which he had fitted with great care all his brother had left behind in the way of information. As she stood waiting Simsa thought she knew what he would ask for next. She put her hand protectingly over that "picture" which she had wrapped in a sheet of thin pro-tective stuff which had been rolled and cased to protect the mist balls. That was hers—she would not give it up. Thom glanced at her, perhaps he read her determination, for he did not ask her to return it. Rather he picked up the now lightless lamp, setting its broad base on the package he had fastened, carefully fitting it into place.

At first Simsa did not quite realize the significance of

his act. Then she took a long stride forward to stand beside him.

"You leave this so—because you believe we shall not return?"

"I believe nothing!" he retorted impatiently. "I only do what is customary."

"One man," she said, "went from this camp and you think died."

He did not answer. She needed no answer. Still her confidence was not shaken. There was always death. If one feared that constantly one had no time for life. One had this day—that was enough to concern one's thoughts.

They left the camp, Zass perched sleepily on Simsa's pack, each of the other two zorsals on a shoulder. When Thom had offered to take their weight, she explained that they would not go to him, nor to anyone else.

The way was smooth enough walking and her well calloused feet had been rested, renewed and strengthened by the pool. He need not fear that she could not keep up with him, and she told him so.

Their door out of the huge chamber of the dome came soon enough, another passage opening to their left. Thom entered without question, Simsa a step or so behind. This was so short a way that the light ahead, which was now sun bright, showed her once more those statues leaning outward from the wall which had given her such a fright the night before. She looked at each eagerly, hoping to discover some resemblance to her picture—but these were like the faces on the upper walls. A number were beasts of one kind or another, none she recognized, only that they seemed to be uniform in that they all showed fangs, claws, or gave the impression of being about to leap upon and slash down some weaker prey.

Three were humanoid, the faces bland, expressionless, with eyes which were mere ovals of smoothed stone. Yet she did not like them. The hostility portrayed by the beasts was open and honest. These others were masks which, she suspicioned, had they been living things, hid emotions and desires more subtle and far worse.

Beyond the passage was another wide space—a road or street. No slippery cobbles set here. The rain had washed across blocks longer than Simsa's height were she to lie full length upon them, still so closely knit together that though there was a crack here and there through which some thread of greenery had fought its way still the pavement was better kept that any of her home city. This highway was bordered on both sides again by tangles of lush greenery from which there arose buildings, three, four, even five stories high, slitted windows like tears along their sides.

Any walks which must have once led to these doors were long since lost in the luxuriant growth, and vines hugged the walls, forming thick cloaks for a good portion of their heights. Simsa thought that it would surely take the flames of the off-world weapon to clear a path to any of them. Thom had brought that with them, still steadying it on his hip, one handed.

"Why not take that off since it will not allow you to use the flame thing?" she asked at last, nodding to the cuff.

"Because I cannot—short of cutting it," he returned quietly. "I have tried."

With a sudden stab of uneasiness she turned the ring on her thumb, found it moved easily enough, that she could withdraw it and return it. Then she plucked at the necklace and it also hung free. Why the off-worlder could not shed his portion of her spoil she did not understand.

His "I cannot" had been short and sharp, making plain that he did not want to speak further of the matter. Still she might have persisted, when, suddenly, he made a quick stop, a half turn, to face the eternal mass of growth which stood between them and the buildings. At the same time she heard, above the noise of insects to which her ears had now become accustomed, another sound, a clicking.

"That way—" Thom started straight ahead for a wall of tangled brush and vine where Simsa could not distinguish a single opening. Then, as they closed in until the nodding ends of vines, seeking new supports, fluttered near them, she caught glimpses of withered growth, a blackened and scorched tree trunk. Someone had used fire to cut a path through here. Now Thom fingered the rod he had carried so carefully.

From the end of that shot a brilliant, searing ray. The vegetation became ash, floating through the air. They had a narrow opening before them. What had grown there was but a screen of brush, for open to them now stood the arch of a door which had been completely hidden by vegetation, which now would begin to hide their own passing.

"You say," Simsa said, as she pressed along on his very heels, having a very unpleasant feeling that the vines and shrubs might begin to close in with an effort to take them prisoner. "You carry a weapon that is not allowed; how did your brother clear this path if he had no such weapon?"

"Well asked," Thom commented. "But if he came the same way we did he may have found that flitter and perhaps, the same as I, a flamer lost by the dead."

"By the guardians?" It would be long before she forgot those suited figures.

Thom's answer was a grunt which meant nothing. He had stepped into a room with painted walls, though there was little light to see those because of the masking of the windows by the growth. Now he switched on his belt light to sweep the beam slowly across the nearest wall.

The paintings were faded but still the colors were visible. They showed odd, asymmetrical arrangements of flowers, and some flying things with brightly spotted wings. The zorsals, now out of the full light, seemed to waken from the stupor which had held them since they had come to Simsa earlier. The two on her shoulders suddenly took wing, up towards the high ceiling. One of them uttered a hunting hoot and swooped into a far corner. What he carried when he arose again made the girl flinch.

"No!" Simsa cried out as the ray of light caught and pinned the zorsal. The thing which he carried, clinging to the prey with his hind paws as he twisted off the head expertly with the front, was only too well known to the girl. What if? She caught at Thom's arm.

"That thing feeds upon the dead," she said in a low voice, which yet sounded far too loud in this chamber. He gave her a slight shove which moved her away.

"Stay!" He mouthed that order even as he strode away. Simsa this time was willing to obey.

She saw Thom's ray of light strike into the corner, hold steady for a long moment. Then the off-worlder was returning.

"Whoever it was wore Guildman's clothing."

The answer was so different from what she expected, perhaps from what he had also expected to discover, that they stood staring at one another.

"One of those who might have followed your brother?"

"Who will ever know now? Come!" The pace he set as he crossed the chamber was close to a lope. Simsa called the zorsals but she knew that they would not return to her until their hunting hunger was satisfied. Under another arch man and girl went, and then they were confronted with a long flight of stairs leading upward.

Simsa was not used to climbing such, but the treads were nearly as low and broad as those they had descended into the place of the pool. They reached a level finally to which the vegetation had not yet grown and light came through the windows. There were no designs on the walls here but they had once been painted a plain golden color in which small specks of glitter sparkled tantalizingly as if marking corners of gem stones near buried from sight.

Another arch brought them out, above a sea of green, to walk a narrow bridge which had been built high in the air. Simsa clutched at a railing. To be so out in the air made her feel dizzy, as if she would begin soon to sway from side to side, as the boat had swayed in the hold of the sea, to topple over the edge, and then fall and fall until the ocean of green below would swallow her forever.

Thom appeared to think this way of traveling entirely natural and was thudding on, never even looking back to where she clung to her anchorage. She set her teeth together and went forward, lest he vanish and be lost in that other building she could see ahead. *He* might be following that off-world guide which would take him along his brother's marked path, but she had none such to keep her from some wrong turning. For here, even the zorsals (within these tombs of buildings) might become lost.

She had to let go of the rail. Fastening her eyes on

Thom's disappearing back, she set out after him at a pace which fear increased even as she went.

They did gain the next building without missteps. Thom stood within the entrance there, that disc once more in his hand, his eyes intent upon it. Simsa had expected to be led to another stair, to descend perhaps as far as they had climbed. Rather, the off-worlder wheeled, passed into a second room, going straight to a window there which was wider than the slits which lay farther down these walls.

He pushed himself up on the ledge to look out and down. Simsa could not see past the width of his shoulders and he said nothing, did not move. At last she could stand the suspense no longer.

"What is it?" She reached out to catch at the arm which wore the cuff, pull at the sleeve so tightly molded against the flesh.

"The end of a world, perhaps." His words meant very little, but he moved aside so that she could look down in turn.

Almost she cried out, but not quite. Then his hand slid across her lips as an additional seal upon secrecy.

Here there was no forest of green—instead a strip so wide its outer edges were almost lost to sight. In places it was blackened, scarred. While on it—

At first she thought they looked down upon a star ship landing field which a fleet in port—a fleet of more ships than had ever come to Kuxortal in a season—in two seasons. Then she saw that most of these ships did not stand erect as if they had landed, as was customary, fins down, noses sky pointed. Two had fallen on their sides, plainly great damaged. Beyond them was a third which was of an entirely different shape altogether than that of the small traders she knew, a round globe from under which protruded a congealed mass of metal: a second ship upon which it had crashed. None of them were—

But, yes, there was one still standing, stark, sky saluting, some distance away. Its sides were smooth and clean where there were the marks of fire, wounds cutting across the others. It looked as if it would be ready to take off at any moment.

But if this was a graveyard for star ships which could no longer fly, it was not deserted. Simsa saw what could only be men, men who wore suits like the dead guardians, but who moved, if clumsily. Several sat on carts which went apparently on their own power from one of the wrecked ships to another. Others walked, so slowly in those heavy body coverings, to pile things they had brought out of the wrecks, sorting them.

Thom's arm shot out. He was holding the strip which he had told her meant the level of death which lay in such places. She could see that red line, which had been near the middle of the strip when he had first shown it to her, was now a finger-width farther up.

"A deadly place."

His voice was low, as if he were awed or shocked by the scene they watched.

"But they—"

"Are suited," he pointed out. "Still, so much danger; what could be worth such exposure?"

"Your weapons of fire?"

"Not just to trade to any little lordlings here," he returned. "Nor could your Lord Arfellen (though I have some idea he knows something of this) dare to come near what is being gathered. This is what is left of a war command."

"Your war—did some of your people flee after all their cities were destroyed?"

He was shaking his head. "These are not ships I know, and they are so old—maybe even Forerunner!"

His eyes were wide. "Forerunner arms! Yes! There would be fools on half a hundred worlds who would pay high for such knowledge, even if they could not touch the weapons themselves. You see these can be taken apart, studied, their ways of making taped. *Then* those who made this find—a find that would be blasted into nothingness if it were public knowledge—would have something to sell such as has never been sold before! *This* is a treasure of evil past any reckoning. We have found burned-off planets, but never before a fleet—or even one ship—which fought such wars! Arms to be studied and copied, the ships themselves. These looters can find buyers in plenty and it will mean ruin and death around the galaxy!"

"What will you do?" The force of his words made each come like a small blow. She could understand what he meant. Those working below would take apart these ancient ships and their arms of horror, learn, sell that knowledge. Who on Kuxortal could stop them, when to even go near that ghostly fleet meant death without protection such as only the enemy had?

13.

Thom turned away from the window, once more showing Simsa a closed face. His hands curled into fists, though the fingers of one were still tight about the off-world weapon.

"What will *I* do?" he repeated softly. He strode two steps across this chamber, turned abruptly and came back to her, to look down at Zass.

"I asked you once before," he said slowly, as if he were thinking his way from one half tangled and unclear part-idea to the next, "what will these do at your ordering." Now he nodded at Zass.

"How would you use them?" she countered quickly. To turn her creatures loose on those men below, who were not only completely enclosed in armor suits but were also working, if what Thom said was true, in an atmosphere deadly to those without protection, was not to be considered.

Thom was back again at the window, gazing at that scene of activity.

"There is a signal, a way to call for help into space, in that wrecked flyer back there," he said. "If it is not damaged and it could be taken out there and set in the midst of that field . . ."

229

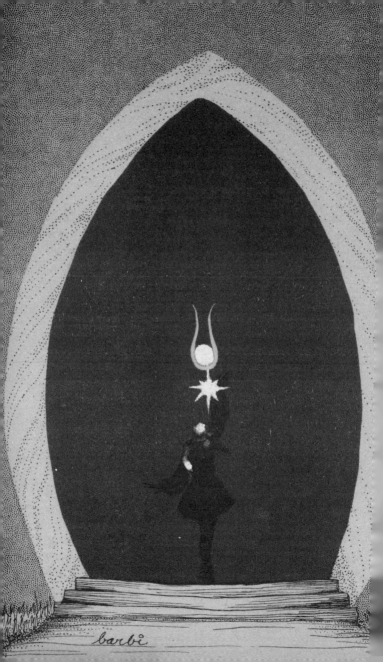

barbi

"Who would hear it?" she demanded. "Do you have a fleet out among the stars waiting for such a call?"

Now he did turn his head to look at her. "When I came here there were those of my service who were suspicious. We reported our mission to the Patrol. This world is a call-stop mainly for Free Traders, smaller ships who deal on their own, captain and crew sharing in the profits. However, it is known that through the years Jack ships—pirates—have set down here and sold their takes, gathered supplies and wares which were legal. There has been a watch on Kuxortal for some seasons now for that reason. Thus there will be a Patrol scout on orbit soon." He hesitated and frowned. "It may already be there. But it will not touch planet until there is a signal broadcast to bring it down. If we could set up a warn-call—"

Simsa smoothed Zass's fine fur. Suppose that the zorsals could be led to do as he wished—and they died of this plague? What did she care for the concerns of his League if such action meant death for these who trusted her?

"It might be done at night," he was continuing. "But also success depends on many factors—whether the signal in the flitter is still usable, whether it can be planted out there, whether I could code in the right call—"

"And whether," Simsa broke in fiercely, "I am willing to send my zorsals to their deaths! You say that men will die down there if they do not wear those suits; what of these?" She held Zass closer against her, heard anxious twitters and chirps from the two males now drawn to them and fluttering about her head.

"If they go swiftly in and out . . ." but his gaze no longer met hers squarely. Then he added explosively: "I can see no other way, and this MUST be done! Would you see your world die in fire? For I tell you that such as would loot this place of the devices here would make very sure that no one else might come to pick through what they may have missed. They will not have long to make such choices—even in their suits they dare not be exposed to radiation so long as it would take to pick clean each and every one of those ships. What they take will be the richest loot. The rest they shall destroy—and to destroy with the weapons they will loose will leave a sore from which poison shall spread to kill and kill!"

"Your plan all depends upon chance and fortune," Simsa answered him. "Even if this other wreck of a flying thing has what you need, will it not be too old to work?" She did not know how much of what he said she could believe. Perhaps he thought he told her the truth, but perhaps also he was mistaken, or trying to frighten her into blindly following any action he planned.

"That much we can make sure of." Again he flung away from the window as if he were impelled, an arrow released from a tight bowstring. He was already heading back and did not even pause to see if she followed. She did reluctantly, uneasy. Were his warnings true? Would those men working below either destroy the ancient ships when they had looted them or would they perhaps give flaming arms to those of the Guild who might have discovered what they did? It would be safer for them to slay out of hand any Lord Arfellen sent; they need not fear any trouble from the Guild, so far away and thus unable to learn what had happened until too late.

Once more she crossed that bridge, striving only to keep her eyes ahead, not to look down. Back they went, until they came again to the camp. Thom lingered for some little time there, turning out boxes and making a selection of things.

It was when they came into the open space, passing once more the tumbled, dead guard, that the off-worlder spoke to her. He had been silently intent on what he was doing and until then did not even seem to note that she was still with him.

He shrugged off his back pack but he did not put down that sack he had filled at the camp.

"Wait here," he ordered. "There is radiation around that flitter—but, as I have said, not enough to cause *me* trouble."

He was off again, squeezing by the standing dead, heading into that part of the ruins from which he had come at their earlier meeting here. Simsa sat down, shrugging off her pack in turn. She rummaged in it for another can of the off-world food. As she opened that Zass and her two sons crowded up against the girl's knees, their forepaws stretched out, making small beseeching sounds. Already they were in thrall to these new tastes and flavors.

The contents of this can were more solid so Simsa broke off bits, sharing them with her companions who chattered loudly and grabbed, to stuff pawsful into their mouths until the cheeks bulged out alarmingly.

She did not like her thoughts. There were far too many ifs in the plan which the off-worlder had so quickly decided upon—*he* had decided. Not her. She still had a choice. The zorsals would never obey any order from him, for which fact she was very glad. That gave her a small chance to keep them safe.

That she could persuade the two males to carry a thing, if it were small and light enough for them to lift, down into that field of dead ships—yes, she believed that could be done. At night they might well be able to do so—unless the suited men kept glare lights on which would half-blind and confuse her creatures. Only what if there was no patrol ship to answer? And what could one ship do? And . . . and . . .? Simsa shook her head, striving to settle her own thoughts into reasonable order.

Put it out of mind, think about something else, for awhile. That was what Ferwar used to counsel when one was frustrated by some problem. Ferwar had always been so eager to collect her bits of the past, poring over them: the carvings, the bits of writing, the two treasures Simsa had brought with her. She felt within her jacket now, closed fingers about the jeweled pendant. But those fingers also brushed against the block and she pulled out that "picture."

In the light of day some of the details were plainer. The girl studied the other Simsa after tipping out the rest of the contents of the food can for the zorsals to squabble over and snatch in enjoyment.

That scar on the skin. Simsa pulled loose her inner belt and turned down the front of her pants to inspect her own smooth lower belly. Save that she lacked that, this was she! Thom had said that his brother had left knowledge of where he had found that from which this had been copied by more of the off-world magic. If she had only made Thom tell her how to get there! The place of dead ships—yes, that was of strangeness and perhaps of account as he kept saying. But *this* was of account to her!

The more she stared at the block, into the eyes of the Simsa imprisoned there, the surer the girl became that she must see, must know. Thom had the belt guide his brother had left. She was certain that he would not yield that up for anything.

There was a city here, many, many tall buildings—she

could search and for maybe five seasons and never come upon the place she desire. But she must *KNOW!*

Was this Simsa a great lady—one who had ruled here among these very broken walls? Or was she, as Thom had mentioned in his stories, one who had also come from the stars at a time so far in the past that even the stones of Kuxortal could not remember? If so—why had Simsa been born to wear her skin, her hair, her body, so many ages later? Blood-tie Thom had said, but what kind of blood-tie could persist through uncounted marches of time?

The girl wished that the Old One was alive, that she could show her this. She wished she had been more demanding of Ferwar's knowledge, pulling answers from the Old One as to why she had been born among the Burrows, who was her mother, her father. Why, oh, why had she not learned more when she could?

Simsa held the long pendant of the necklet into the full light comparing the gems in it, the way it was set, with that jeweled fringe about the "pictured" hips. This was no pendant! It had been part of a like kilt such as the woman in the cube wore. That was why it was in the form of a long strip . . . .

The cuff? No, the Simsa in the block did not wear one of those, nor did she have a ring like that on the girl's thumb. Still Simsa was sure that both other pieces had a place in the same time and world as that of the "pictured" figure.

She was excited, restless. Then she remembered that box which Thom had stowed so carefully under the beacon at the camp. There might be something there—something which would give her the answer. There was no reason why she should not go to look!

Catching up Zass, the other two zorsals taking to wing over her head, Simsa skirted the fallen dead man, made her way back to the camp.

With care she lifted the lamp from the box, half fearing that she might in some way set it to burning. Then she pressed the lid of the container as she had seen Thom seal it. There were what he had called "tapes"—of no use to her. Under them some more of the blocks such as that she had taken for her own.

Each held a small, three dimensional object. The first was a wreck—Simsa eyed that carefully, and decided that it was much smaller and of an entirely different shape than those she had seen scattered about the field. Perhaps this was of that "flitter" which Thom had now gone to examine.

In the next was a doorway—not a plain opening such as they had passed through to get into the building from which the bridge in the sky had led. No, there was vegetation here which had been torn away, but the door itself was arched, with a broad band of color—or rather colors, one blending with the other in subtle combinations and shades—running completely about that arch from the pavement on one side to that on the other.

What was more important to the girl was that this archway was not open. It had a door across it and in the middle of that barrier, showing very plain in the representation was the symbol of what Thom called "Sun-and-Moon" horns about the ball, even as the Simsa "picture" carried and wore.

Did this place stand somewhere within the ruins about her? Simsa pawed through the other blocks—there were three more. One of them was of the pool curtained by mist; this she discarded at once. Another seemed to portray a long section of wall on which ran lines of carving—some ancient record—of no use to her, and that also she dropped. However, the third, like that of the doorway, was meaningful.

It might have been fashioned by someone looking down a great chamber or room. The same colors which had played about the doorward were laid on here in wavering bands along the walls but only part way down the length of what Simsa believed was a long hall.

The colors ended abruptly in an expanse of silvery gray—a color which held both the sheen of the pool sand and the opaque beauty of the cupped liquid. This surrounded a dais on which stood—Simsa gave a small cry of eagerness; smaller indeed than the other picture she had treasured, but the same!—here stood that other one, her other self!

Out there, somewhere among the ruins there was a doorway and beyond that—this! She need only seek and she would find! Stowing those three blocks in her sleeve pocket, she hurriedly repacked the box to put it under the lamp, trying to replace all even as she had found it. Let the off-worlder worry about his wrecks and those who looted them, she had this which belonged to her alone, the secret which had become the most important thing in her life. Enough prudence remained for her to catch up and don her pack.

Then, with Zass perched on the pack, her head bobbing forward so that her mouth was not far from Simsa's ear, the other two zorsals overhead, the girl padded out once more to that road which ran through the vine and shrub shrouded ruins in search of the doorway—and of what lay beyond it.

The two male zorsals winged over her head. She wished that she could convey to them what she sought, but to show them the picture, ask them to find that arch—that was too complicated. She must depend upon fortune and her own two feet and persistence.

Simsa realized that the sprawl of ruins was far larger than she had first believed, as there seemed no end to the road, to the buildings which arose on either side. Her impatience grew but her determination did not falter. Somewhere here lay what she sought—the belief in that waxed stronger instead of less, despite the fact that she had found not a single sign of anyone passing the way before her.

The zorsals whirled in and out among the buildings. There were large insects which took to the air on lacy, near invisible wings, or on those which were dotted and splotched with vivid color which shone even brighter against the green of the plants from which they came. Still there was silence here.

Simsa went slowly, for as she passed each of the buildings she looked for signs that the vegetation had been burnt back, that someone had gone this way before her. There were trees growing tall, shading many of the lower stories of the buildings, so choked with vines tying one to the other that it was difficult to imagine that even a flame weapon could burn a path here.

The road curved to the right, in the direction of that distant landing field. Simsa, eager as she still was, drew closer now to the growth near to hand. Had some of those looters already come this way, or were they so intent on what they had found among the wrecked ships that this city meant nothing to them? She could not be sure.

A greater twist of curve, almost the road appeared to

be turning back, curling on itself. Still she could see that it had an end. Narrowed, it led straight to—

Simsa's breath caught. She stood, small, dwarfed and made insignificant by that before her. Here was her door of colors! But it was an arch so tall and—

Her hand flew to her mouth, she found that she was pressing that thumb ring painfully tight against her lips as her head went farther back and she looked up and up—and up.

This was a building, not for men, but for some intelligence, some race, who were more than men—more at least than men of the kind she knew. Also it was totally different from the city in which it stood.

The city was old, Simsa had no doubt of this, but here within it was something far older yet. This held no kinship to the other buildings. There were no vines, no shrubs, no trees to veil it, and it was kin to the towered ring—truly it was!

From the ring to those grey-white walls which also held a blue sheen, Simsa looked and looked again. There seemed to spread outward from it, from that gateway framed in the band of entwined color, a chill, a breath of such age as Simsa half expected to see it crumble and be gone to dust even as she walked slowly toward it. She could no more have turned aside now than she could take to the air as the zorsals had.

Three wide steps led to that door. Simsa climbed those, the towered keep rearing above her as might a crouching beast. That carving she had sold to Thom—animal body, half human head. Now she stood before the door on which that symbol of X-Arth (or perhaps more than X-Arth; fragments of what Thom had said flitted through her mind) shone with a pale silver radiance.

Her ringed hand went out. She must open that door, though somewhere, deep in her mind, some small uneasiness fought vainly to keep her from it. No—this was what she was *meant* to do. Old, old—forgotten—not wholly. She was breathing faster, her heart raced. Fear, awe, and something else fastened on her, made her one to be used, without any will of her own.

Her fingers touched the door well below that symbol, for the door was so tall she would have had to stand on tiptoe to touch even the lower edge of that. She planted her palm against the surface, expecting it to be cold as the stone in which it was set. But it was as if she touched a thing through which flowed energy. The gem on her ring sparked with a sudden explosion of colors, near matching those about the arch so high now over her head.

The door moved, swinging wide, though she had exerted no pressure, only touched it. Simsa passed within.

Here—here was the huge hall-chamber of that other picture. She was only partly aware that the colors along these walls seemed to actually move, flow ceaselessly one into another, lighter to darker, darker to lighter. It was what stood in the center of that place facing her, though a long space lay between them, which centered her whole attention.

Simsa took a step, flinched—

Though she could see nothing, it was as if some cold, repelling mist hung before her, chilling her. There was such a darkness, not before her eyes, but within her. Yet she was also drawn. Without her willing it her be-ringed hand began to move, sweeping forth, and then from side to side, as if she lifted unseen curtains, clearing a passage through the intangible.

Step by step she went. Fear blackened the world about

her, her heart beat so fast now that she felt it shake in her body, she could hardly breathe. Dimly she knew that she was fighting a barrier, a barrier which in its time had killed and would kill again. Still she could not retreat. That which waited drew her on.

It was a journey which might have lasted for hours, even days—here was no time as man measured it, only a war between two parts of her—one which was stricken with fear, one which yearned and drove her on. She did not know that she was crying, that small sobs from pain which was not of her body marked her torment. She was being wrung in two. And she knew that if she lost either part, if there was separation, then she would have failed—and that which was truly Simsa would cease to be.

At last she came to stand at the foot of the dais, looking up at the other who was she—or who was the essence of a race from which she had been drawn. Her arm fell limply to her side. That other was gazing down, the eyes were open, were fixed upon hers. Simsa gave a last, small, piteous cry and fell limply at that other's feet, her struggle ended.

Her body twitched, convulsed, a drop of froth trickled from one side of her mouth. She had entered her last defense, a withdrawal deep into her innermost part, abandoning all else to that pressure which assaulted her.

Assaulted her? No, there was no desire to torment, to invade, to—

The girl lay quiet now. She sighed once, turning her head a fraction so that still her eyes met those of the other. Inside her mind barriers weakened, gave away. She was as one who had been in prison all her life and was now suddenly lifted into wide fields under an open sky.

This very freedom was first pain in itself because it brought with it more overwhelming fear.

Her lips shaped pleas to powers—powers—what powers? There was one Simsa, now. Her body lay in birth pangs as her mind and soul formed another. She could not understand, she tried to flee from that act of birth, but there was no going back.

At length she lay, her last defenses breached, the sacrifice, the victim. A last part of the old Simsa cried aloud that this was death—the end—and once more fear fell upon her as a dark cloud.

Through that terror pierced something else, clean, clear, free. She got to her knees, her hands going up and out to catch at the edge of the dais. She was so weak, so young and new, and this was—

Exerting what strength she could summon, Simsa drew herself to her feet, still holding on, for she felt as if the world were atilt and she was about to spin out among the stars . . . . the great suns . . . the planets.

There was a whirling in her head, too, as if memory piled upon memory, though none was clear, and she felt that she was battered until her spirit was as sore as if she were a slave flogged for another's pleasure. Not *her* memories. When had she ever walked among the stars, when had she ever held power in her two hands and ruled a world and then lost that rule through the treachery of time?

She was young, at the beginning, not at the end.

As she clung to that thought, the memories grew smaller, dimmer, were gone, except that now and then a single blurred picture might rise for an instant, to disappear once again. As one who was just born she gazed still up at that other, begging silently for the warm comfort of aid.

Her hands moved over her body, stripping away the outer crust—the wrapping about the new born. Then she stood free of the past—the short and dark past, free, too, of much of the longer past—the bright awesome one. She reached up higher. The tips of her fingers could just touch the end of the rod that other held, that sceptre of power and triumph.

Under that light touch it moved, tilted, slipped, so came into her hold. As she grasped it, so did the change come, nearly in the blink of an eye. She who had been the other, and was now only a husk, vanished as a husk would so when the power which held it together was drawn out of it. What had seemed a living woman became—a statue—leaving behind only that which had been of this world—

With the sureness of one who had done this many times over Simsa reached out to take up in turn what was hers by right—the girdle of gems, the crown chain. As she locked those upon her body she held her head high. By the True Mother, she was Simsa perhaps, but she was also the Daughter who had come into her heritage!

She turned to look back that way which she had come. There would be no barrier there for her now. A honking cry at her feet drew her attention to Zass. Simsa knelt on one knee, pushing aside with a frown of distate the draggled clothing she had shed. She held out her hand and the zorsal came to her, wing dragging.

With the sceptre of power Simsa touched that ill-set wing, drawing the rod along its surface. The wing had become partly healed in the pool; now it wholly straightenend, and Zass fanned it wide, hooting hoarsely.

The power had lasted!

For a moment she was caught again in that whirl of conflicting memories. Simsa brushed her hand across her forehead. No, she must not push against what held her now. All would come right—she need only wait. Wait and act when she knew that the action was ready. This was a time to bide quiet and wait; there would come what was needed to fill her, to nourish her.

She smiled and held the wand against her between her breasts. No, she was not that one who *had* been waiting here through time, but she bore the same blood, was a daughter tossed up from the age flow of this world—perhaps by chance—perhaps through some plan long past. This was where she had been called to be, now she would travel on, returning that which she held in her to be once more woven into the affairs of men and worlds.

Zass took to the air, screaming delight and triumph. The two other zorsals flew to join her as Simsa sat back on her heels and watched their dance of joy. Such small ones, so strong in their own ways— A world could be fair—it was only with the coming of another species that anger, hate, fear were made to last the length of a day, draw blackness into dreams by night.

The zorsals winged back toward the doorway. Simsa, without a glance at the skin of she who had not yet been born—the grimy clothing, the pack—followed them. That heady joy in life which had filled her when she had lain in the Pool of Renewing (that which had been wrought by a younger and less people who had understood only a little of true knowledge) was raised, flooded through her.

She threw her arms wide, half expecting to see the light of power flame from each of her wide-spread fingers. Though it did not show, yet it was there. And she was only newly born—there was much to learn, to understand, to be.

Simsa passed under the gate into the open. The sun was low in the sky, hanging over the ruins of the city. If she wished she could call to mind who had dwelt there once for so long, the dusty burden of their history. But that no longer mattered—it was gone past and there was no reason to draw such back. For it was the same history as all men faced, as all intelligent species faded. It had a slow beginning, it arose to pride and triumph, it fell to defeat and decay. It—

Simsa whirled about, the gems of her kilt fringe flashing. She stood, her nostrils expanding as if she could pick up danger by scent. Not scent, no, that alarm had come to her through the very air which pressed now against her body. There was danger . . . there—

Again she half pivoted, as if her body were part of an intricate device—her sceptre turned and pointed now into the ruins to her left.

14.

A figure moved, came into the open where the declining rays of the sun were already overshadowed, cut by the buildings around. Simsa shook her head, trying to so throw off that mixture of memories. Death had walked so, once.

There was another behind the first, a grotesque creature as if one of the carvings of stone had come to life to clump along on clumsy feet. Simsa's nostrils expanded again. The three zorsals above her head gave tongue, started to fly towards those two who were coming. Then with a burst of their highest speed, they cut away, even as that clumsy, stumping, second invader sprayed the air with a blast of flame.

Anger was born, cold and clear, in Simsa. Her glow of happiness and freedom was wiped away in an instant. She pointed with the sceptre. From the twin horn tips which were a part of that ancient sign of the Great Mother-One shot in return glittering spears of light, no thicker than her finger but potent, drawing briefly from her anger and strength.

Together those struck full on the weapon, that black, flame caster held by the suited one. There was a burst of white, a flare near blinding in its intensity. He who had

247

fired upon the zorsals stood still. His captive had thrown himself flat even as she had raised the sceptre, now he rolled—a maneuver which carried him behind a fallen column broken in its length across the open way.

Simsa, feet braced apart, stood wary and waiting. Now she could see clearly that one who was suited even as had been the dead "guardians", the men who had been at work in the landing field among the wrecked ships.

She caught her lower lip between her teeth. That flare of energy had been drawn from her own reserves of energy of body and mind. She was not yet ready to fight so—she could not summon strength for another such attack. There was so much which she must learn, must practice. She was still too caught by the Simsa she had lately been, fettered in spirit, clouded in mind—not what life had intended her species to be.

Still, that suited one did not advance. While his weapon— The girl saw what he held, a lump melded into his metal-protected hands—a stump, which still radiated heat, a heat she could feel even from this distance. The power of the Horns had turned back upon him the force of his own vicious weapon. So in a manner he had brought his own fate upon himself. She did not know he was dead, only that he was no longer a threat.

The prisoner he had taken appeared to understand this, also. He arose from where he had taken cover during that exchange of energies. For a long moment he half turned, to view the motionless suited figure, then he looked to Simsa, his eyes once more opened to their widest extent, an expression of complete amazement giving away slowly to a just as astounded recognition.

Simsa walked forward, drawing into her by will alone, after a manner which she could not yet understand but which was as natural as breathing, energy from the air about. Perhaps even the dregs of that which had been expended in combat here came to feed her at her need. For with each step her strength increased. There was no sound, even the zorsals held silence, no sound but the faint musical ring of the gemmed strings she wore.

"Simsa—?" Thom had fully turned from his captor. His calling of her name was not quite recognition, rather his tone held a note of question, as if he knew that he saw her, still was not sure of the truth of what came towards him.

"Simsa." She made answer of her name. That was not a name out of that far dim past. However, that did not matter. In this time and place she was Simsa and was willing that that should be so.

He came slowly towards her, still studying her with that intent stare. She pointed over his shoulder, to the suited one.

"This is one of the looters? They know what you would do?"

He gave a start, as if she had shaken him abruptly from one line of thought to another.

"They had a persona detect working—it picked up radiation from the signal when I brought that within their range. Also it proclaimed I was a stranger, not coded into their company. Having that they can hunt us down—"

"That one—" she tilted the sceptre a fraction towards the motionless, suited invader, "is he dead?"

"With such a back lash he may be. What did you use on him?" Thom demanded eagerly. She guessed that he would have liked to have taken the sceptre into his own hands, to have sought to discover the secret. But that was not for him. He was a man—also he was of another race—a one whose blood flow, whose mind and body, could never feed the right form of energy.

"I used the Power," she said serenely. "Will there be more like this one to come ahunting?"

That question brought his attention back to the here and now. He looked over his shoulder. This much closer she could see that, not only was the weapon that invader had carried reduced to a fused mass of metal, but the whole forefront of his protective suit was blackened. Various other blobs which must have hung from just such a belt as Thom wore were also sealed as useless knobs to the suit itself.

"Yes."

Simsa considered what might lay before them. She had used the Power this time without truly realizing what it might cost. Now she instinctively knew that she could not bring it into battle again until she had regained more of the life force upon which it drew. This thing out of time was not meant for sustained battle—for the defeat of men. Rather for healing— for . . . she did not yet know just all it might do. That, too, was part of what she must learn by very careful experimentation, drawing upon a part within herself which had just been born into life, a kind of life she might have never conceived existed before this had happened to her.

"I cannot defeat such again." She must make that fact plain to him. "There is a limit placed upon this. What would you do?"

He was versed in weapons and battle; this problem was to be solved by his kind of knowledge, not hers.

Thom moved closer, still eyeing her as if he sought to learn some secret from the way her hair moved slightly at the tug of the evening breeze, from the way she met him eye to eye. She could sense the need in him for the asking of questions, but also there was the greater need for action.

"I have—I had—the signal," he spoke rapidly, breaking that bond of gaze between them, as if he must free himself in so little, in order to return to the pressure put upon him by what he considered his duty. "But I do not think that they know of the upper way we found to see the landing fields. Perhaps that one," he nodded at the suited figure, "is a scout who picked up the signal, so came to investigate. He took me before I reached the building—"

"And the signal?"

"Back there in the bushes. It must be planted. If they take off before it is—"

"Yes," it was her turn to understand. "Death will follow—not only on this world, but spreading outward, as do rings when a stone is dropped into a pool. Save that this stone is potent poison and an ending for all. There have been such endings before, doubtless there will be more to come. For their species is cursed with this greed, for domination, for the dealing of death."

Simsa spoke out of another stir of broken memory—then sealed it quickly from her mind. She must rather think clearly of what faced them.

"Will there be time to do as you have planned?" she asked then.

Thom shrugged. "Who knows? But one must try."

"Always one tries," she echoed as memory also echoed, far and faint.

She whistled to the zorsals, softly. Zass wheeled, came to her, the two males flanking their dam on either side. When all three were just overhead, circling above Simsa and Thom, she spoke again:

"Let us go there to where you left the signal."

She did not look at the suited one again. If the Power had added a third dead guardian to this city of the long dead, she did not want to know or remember her part in that act.

"Where did you get that?" Thom pointed to the sceptre. His strides were no longer difficult for her to match, as they sped down the wide avenue between the vine shrouded buildings.

"I found Simsa," she returned briefly. "I am now—whole." That was the surprising truth. She had been empty before, part of her missing, her mind stunted, narrow, unable to perceive what was of importance, though there had been an unrecognized ache in her ever for what was missing. How such as she had come into this world—what chance of birth had brought her body to match that of the Forgotten, that she might never know. However, she did understand that at last, her mind, her inner self, was now united with that body, fitting one part to another as it should always have been.

She knew he still eyed her, waiting for her to say more. Only there was no desire in her to share what had happened to her. Still, it was because of him—or his brother—that this wonder, this fulfillment had come to her. Perhaps so she owed him no small debt.

"I found other 'pictures' which your brother left. They led me to Simsa."

"The image! But T'seng reported on his tape there was an energy barrier of some sort—that he could not get close. Even that picture you claimed first had to be taken with a distant vision charger—"

He spoke of off-world things which did not matter. So

perhaps that Simsa *had* been guarded until the proper time came. The girl remembered dimly how she had had to force her way through an invisible web to reach the place she had been meant to stand. But then she had been unknowing, another person. So the web guarded until the time was ripe, until the true blood returned to claim—

Once more the confusion of too-full memory struck at her. She resolutely broke that train of thought quickly.

"There was something. Yes. I could not see, though it tried to hold me back. But still I went on—to her."

"T'seng believed that place to be Forerunner, older than the city. The statue—you are now wearing—" He glanced at her meager adornment, then quickly away as if she might resent his eyes so upon her. Why should she? Her body was a part of her, even as was her speech, her thoughts. There was no reason to hide behind such grimed shells as she had worn before. Simsa thought with fleeting distaste of having such once more covering her own skin.

"There was no statue," she replied remotely. "There was Simsa and I am Simsa. She waited until I came. Now we are free."

He smiled ruefully. "Not for long if these Jacks have more trackers out. Though this is a good place to hide," he glanced about at the ruins. "Still we have no time for such games." Now his voice and face were both grim.

They had set a good pace and had rounded the curve of the avenue which led away from the castle-keep which was like her ring. The girl could see ahead the wall of that place where there were so many seats, and this side of that was the building where Thom's brother had left his trail markers.

"Wait!" Thom flung up his arm, but she had already caught that movement in the green beyond. No evening wind had stirred as vigorously as that! There was an ambush—

Simsa raised her hand, drew the zorsals to a tight formation just above her with a gesture. Together with Thom she darted swiftly to the left, where they crouched together now in cover, seeking a hunt of what waited beyond.

"How many?" the girl wondered aloud.

"Can your zorsals discover that?" Thom asked. "I no longer have the beamer. We cannot stand up to any weapon of theirs. This stuff—" He moved his hand slowly so as not to cause any betraying quiver of the vegetation around them, "is too thick for us to force a path through."

Simsa held out one hand, the other still clutched the sceptre which was the most precious thing on this world she realized without being told. Zass slipped between two vines, coasted down, to alight on the girl's shoulder.

She turned her head a fraction so she might stare straight into the huge eyes of the zorsal. Almost she cried out. It was as if she had suddenly opened a book such as the Guild Lords were known to treasure. She was looking *in*. Before her lay an alien mind. Thought paths would clear for an instant or two, and then haze over, so that Simsa lost touch. Still in its way this other mind was complete, keen, knowing—

She had no time for exploration, all she could do was to look into those eyes and *think*. Zass uttered a very low, guttural agreement to that thought, before slipping away on four feet, wings furled, held tight to her body.

"What she can learn," Simsa reported to the off-worlder, "she will. Only I shall not let my small people be caught in that death-fire!"

He was watching her again with that wide-eyed astonishment. "What happened? You—you are—"

"I am Simsa," she told him firmly for the second time. "Your brother was right in this. Those of my blood once knew the stars—this world but one among many. Time is not to be counted by those who voyage so. A sleep, an awakening, a coming, a going, a lapping out, a drawing in. Once such voyaging was for us—now it is for you." She slipped the sceptre from hand to hand. "Memory is a burden to which I cannot now submit. I am Simsa and I live. I do not care to know the why of that. Ah."

It was not Zass who returned in the same devious way that his dam had left, but one of the males. He squatted down before Simsa, staring up into her face. She reached out with the wand and touched him, where the wings joined his shoulders, with the two horn tips. He gave a small croon.

His mind was not so open. She could only read small, distorted fragments, but enough.

"There are four who wait. They have found that which you brought, but they have left it as bait. They are very sure of capturing you—us."

"Four," he repeated wryly. Her mind took another path, disregarding the strength of the opposition.

"This signal of yours, how large is it?"

He stretched forth his hands to measure a space as long as the zorsal before her was tall.

"How heavy?" she demanded next.

"About—well, I can lift it with one hand. They were made compact, you see. Sometimes they had to be set by men who were injured or who otherwise could not manage to shift heavy weights."

Simsa caught her lower lip between her teeth, thinking, easily and quickly, as if she saw exactly what must be done laid out before her as one of those "pictures" which had led her to Simsa.

"The box that you say nullified the pull of the earth." Fleetingly she realized that she now understood exactly *what* he had meant, though her new flash of understanding was of no matter. "That lies still on the carrier?"

"No," he opened a distended pouch at his belt to show her the box. "I thought it was not wise to leave it."

"This thing can be in some way attached to your signal?" She was groping as well as hoping; the plan which seemed so clear to her would fail for just such a lack.

"Yes." He turned the box around to show her a small indentation in its surface. "Put this against what must be raised, press this, and the force is activated."

She dared to rise a little in their hideout to glance beyond leaves and branches to the sky. The low sun was already shut off by the buildings. Shadows now not only lengthened but also darkened across the ground.

"Give me this!" Before he could deny her, Simsa caught the box from out of his hand, taking care not to bring it near the sceptre. She looked down at the zorsal, trying to make this thought command as simple as she could. Three times she went through what must be done, until she could read the reflection of her orders within the creature's own mind.

The zorsal snatched the box out of her hands, and, with one fore paw holding it tight against his chest, scrambled back into the greenery. Simsa turned to Thom.

"You asked before if the little ones could carry your signal down into that place, but you said exposure to the poison there might mean death. Therefore they shall take it in their own way. With your nullifier to aid against its weight they shall fly it to the top of one of those dead ships, wedge it there. None of those who loot will, I believe, see them. Nor would those off-worlders search for a signal in the air above them—would they?"

He stared at her. "Your zorsals can do this?" he asked after a moment.

"I believe that they can. At any reckoning it may be the only chance you have, unarmed and with those who watch and wait for you there. Can *you* hope to do as well?"

Thom shook his head. Then he stiffened, but she had also heard a rustling, a snapping of branches, a rattling of vines. Perhaps those in ambush had begun to believe that their plans had gone awry and had sent out one of their number to see why.

The off-worlder's hand flew to his belt. She saw him touch that length of metal which he had said could measure the death breath of the ancient weapons of his kind. On the small strip the light line swung upward. She felt a tingle in her skin but was unafraid. There was no warning alert here but born out of the Simsa-of-the-past's memories.

"Hot—he's hot! Get back!" Thom swept his arm back as if to sweep her away from him.

At the same time a ray of light cut through the green above their heads, started to slice down towards them. Simsa threw herself to the right with that agility by which the other Simsa had learned to defend herself. At the same time she called out from the depths of her new half understanding.

"The cuff! Use the cuff."

He might have thought her urging foolish, but at that moment he did not disdain it. Throwing up his arm across his face toward which that menacing beam swung, he brought the cuff between his head and that death-by-light.

The ray struck and spread across the surface of the cuff, then was radiated, swollen to twice its size, as the energy sent in to blast and kill was fed back along the same path by that defense. It happened in only a few breaths of time, but the reflected force set greenery to smoldering, swept back upon itself with doubled power—a power intended to exterminate helpless prey.

Thom crouched, still holding his arm up. The cuff seemed untouched to the eye by the force feeding back from it, from him to the killer. Simsa fingered the sceptre, longing to use it, yet sure that the off-worlder had a defense which would drain nothing from him in strength and still would save him.

There came a flare, a great clap of noise, with heat to follow. Simsa fell into the midst of a half withered bush, heard a crash from the other side. She clawed her way out of a mass of crushed leaves and spiny twigs, some of which punished her with raking scratches. Thom lay still, his head and shoulders half hidden, his long legs tailing towards her.

On her hands and knees she reached him. His eyes were open, seemingly unfocused for a moment. Then they centered on her, and she saw recognition in them. He raised his arm slowly upward, so that he could look upon the cuff without moving his head.

The ancient artifact was burnished, bright, even in the

shadows here. It even glowed as if the fire which had struck it had supplied or awakened an energy which was truly its own. Still there was no mark upon it of any of the force which it had bent to crisp and kill.

Now Thom did turn his head, look at her. "How, how did you know?" His voice, for the first time she had known him was really shaken, he seemed vulnerable, no longer the superior starman whose people had key to secrets forbidden to the worlds they visited.

"It is one—" she tried now to find words which would explain something which she had not yet sorted out for herself. "That was one of the other Simsa's memories, one of the old defenses."

He put out his other hand as if to run finger tips over the surface of the cuff, but snatched them back before his flesh had touched the unknown metal.

"*You* are Simsa—"

"I am Simsa," she agreed. "Blood of her blood. Though I do not know that came to be, for she was . . . what your brother thought her to be. Long before the coming of those who built this city (and they also have been gone for tens-tens-tens past counting of seasons) she was here. Also she was the last of her people. But in some way she must have planned that there would be one to follow her through time. I do not know how, but I am her child new born. Yet still I am Simsa. But why do we waste time now in talk? One found us. Others will come now to search."

Thom sat up, holding the cuffed arm away from his body as if he still feared to let it touch any part of him.

"You are right." He began to edge backwards, using the growth as cover. As Simsa started to follow there was a shaking in the fire-touched brush. A small sapling crashed forward, falling outward towards the avenue, baring a new wide section to their sight as it came down, tearing half burnt vines with it.

Another of the suited invaders lay there, half covered by the mass that the falling tree had brought down with it, only his legs covered by the thick plating of the suit to be seen. Simsa had no doubt that he was dead. Also she was glad she was unable to see what havoc the return of his own fire had caused.

Thom had suddenly paused, his tense attitude in the gathering shadows one of a listener. There were other rustlings—Thom beckoned to her vigorously, his gesture made more emphatic by the gleam of the cuff which continued to hold a light of its own. She glanced at the sceptre. Yes, there was also a very wan outline of thin light about the symbols at its crown. She held it in front of her, close to her body, feeling a gentle, pulsating warmth from that same set of horns which had unleashed death earlier.

With what skill they could they had somehow found a way to a gaping doorway of one of the buildings. To try for the open avenue was to make them easy targets. The inside of the structure was a dark cavern, even though complete twilight had not closed in, but it was a promise of shelter.

Simsa could see that they had entered a single great room which appeared to fill the entire structure, there was no ceiling above, only a continued rise, though narrowing as it went, for the side walls were a series of steps in the form of balconies, off which were dark openings at regular intervals. The lowest of these was supported by carven pillars much like those they had seen elsewhere, stands of vegetation or monstrous life forms.

Thom had gone to the nearest of these and was running his hands across the deep ridges of the carving. He looked over his shoulder as she joined him.

"These can be climbed. If those Jacks are all suited they can't follow us. The suits are far too clumsy to climb in."

"And if they sit below, waiting for us?"

"At least we shall have a breathing space to plan something."

He was already climbing and she saw that he was right; the deep gouges left by those who had wrought this representation of a vine wreathed tree gave ample space to fit fingers and toes. She took the warmth of the sceptre into her mouth and swung up easily behind him.

They lay side by side on the floor of the first balcony watching the door. Waiting came hard. Simsa again ran the smooth tube of the sceptre back and forth between her hands. However she was firm in keeping a barrier now against wandering memories. In the here-and-now she needed all her awareness for what might happen next, not for what had happened in the long-ago and had no meaning to her at present.

They heard the crunch of heavy footsteps. It was very dark now in the building—there appeared to be no windows at all. Simsa's night sight had adjusted only to the point where she could detect movement at the door gap . . . very cautious movement. Those others must have found the blasted body of their man, be fearing some attack out of the dark.

Whoever had hesitated there for an instant was again gone. Simsa could not tell whether out or in. Thom's shoulder pressed against hers. He had turned his head so that his whisper came so low and close that she could feel the slight pressure of his breath against her cheek.

"They have a body heat detect—a persona. If it is with this party they will know just where we are. They will try to keep us prisoned here until they can bring some stronger weapon out of the loot to finish us off."

If he were trying to prove to her how serious their position might be, she was already well aware of that.

"How long?" she whispered in return. Might they keep on climbing up from one balcony to the next?

No! The answer came to that as a wide beam of light which began a slow sweep around the interior of the huge hall, first at floor level, so each of those pillars, such as the one they had just climbed, stood out in sharp relief. Then at the far end of that sweep, on the opposite side from which they lay, the light arose to the second level. Thom's hand fell heavy between her shoulders, forcing her against the floor.

"Stay flat!"

There was a solid balustrade for the balcony, reaching perhaps the height of her knees were she standing. Simsa wondered if that would be enough of a barrier to hide them both. Or if the seekers below would realize that they might be so concealed and begin an indiscriminate spraying with their flamers—a wild rush of fire they could not hope to guard against.

The light traveled. She had pillowed her head, cheek against her arm, and watched it sweep. Now the beam had nearly reached them, was turning along their side. Simsa realized she had been holding her breath. She had for these tense moments returned to the old Simsa. Her confidence, her feeling of superiority over these clumsy looters had ebbed. The sceptre lay under her hand, but at that moment she could not have released its power even if she would. The sharp danger had swung her to the other side of the balance and she was only a badly frightened girl. That other Simsa—she *must* find her, *be* her again, or she might soon be nothing at all.

15.

Yes, close one's eyes—remember only that Simsa! The Simsa who had stood proud, tall, knowing, unafraid. Do not think of the light moving closer, of alien death by fire, just Simsa.

She willed her heart to slow its beat, she willed fear to be her servant not her master. Even as anger can be willed to become a tool when the time comes, emotions can give greater strengths to one. She *willed*.

There was a sharp pain which ran from her cheek into her head—causing for a moment such agony that she thought hazily the flamers of the hunters had found her. Then the pain vanished as swiftly as it had struck, leaving behind it—

This was a strong return of that same feeling she had known in the hall of that other Simsa—that she was new, that she was now another. Dimly the girl was aware that the hand, clasping the sceptre with a force which made her fingers ache, also lay against her head. The ring—the ring had become a bridge!

How—or why—or what—? All questions which must be pushed aside for now. There was an urgency, a need, to act!

What she was doing was a matter of obeying com-

266

mands, silent commands, delivered from a source she could not define, did not know, who had once been able to do this, and had used such action as a shield and a weapon.

Simsa opened her eyes but did not move her head. She saw the gem which formed the roof of the tower on her ring—saw that only. It grew, spread, became like the pool in which she had lain, became more than the pool—rather a sea. Into that sea she made herself plunge—not the Simsa who was a body, rather the Simsa who dwelt within that body.

She sharpened her thoughts, her purpose, fumbling a little at first, then growing more sure, more adept. There was only the grey-blue-white sea which drew her thoughts, to form them anew, send them out as weapons.

Far away she heard a whisper of sound, a rise and fall of cadence, of the reciting of a ritual in a tongue which had not been spoken for a thousand-thousand lifetimes. There was strength arising from that stream of words, flowing on into her as it grew louder, gathering energy for another in-pouring as it faded again.

Into the waiting sea spilled that force. Its surface was troubled so waves arose—not waves of any liquid, rather surges of power towering higher and higher. So—and so—and *so*—! Yes, this was what must be done, even as it had been evoked long ago. The power in her was still not great enough to move the very earth itself—though once such power had been so used—such cadences of rising and falling words had fitted stones into place, had lifted even great burdens skyward. She did not have that, but her efforts were answering in a different way—answering!

The rising turbulence of that sea closed around the essence of her own identity, caught and held her. She could have screamed aloud as that essence was rent by a tearing, a forcing of dismemberment. Now she was two . . . three . . . .

Two and three—and still one. Simsa marshalled those others, those parts of her—they were her guardsmen, her warriors. Now it was time to send them into battle.

She looked into a great hall. There was no darkness there for her eyes, though she knew that in truth shadows hung heavy and long. Through the dark below things moved.

There was a haze about them. The haze of of energy—two kinds of energy—one came from outward sources, one from inner. It was the inner which was of the greater importance—that source of energy which was born of life force, not from any weapon or rank discovery and foul use by those who meddled in what they could not hope to completely conquer.

Go—so!

Silently she commanded the two which had been born from her own essence, even as she had been reborn out of Simsa of old.

They blazed. They were light itself. And still they were her, night dark of skin, moon silver of hair, with the sign of the Great Mother blazing from head and hand. Two of them stood in the middle of that hall's darkness facing those who came.

The ones clothed in haze halted. She could see the ripple of their inner essence's diffusion which answered to every change of emotion. They were first astounded, then triumphant. One thought death—was moved to sight with his weapon to destroy. Two others quickly defeated his desires. She could hear no orders, but the thought behind their communication rang plain. The two she had dispatched must be taken prisoner.

There they stood. To lay hands upon them, to use an entangling device was a matter of no difficulty. Coils of thin white stuff spun through the air. The coils wreathed around the Simsas. It was meant to pull tight, to wrap them past all struggle for freedom. The coils slipped, fell to the floor where they writhed ineffectively as might living things which had been blinded, or broken.

Now he who had sought to kill from the beginning set his weapon on full strength and, over the protests of his companions, fired. Fire streamed, encircled, blazed with force. Those other Simsas stood unharmed.

There was dismay now. The in-hazed ones were touched by alarm, by uneasy awareness that they fronted something not within the range of their knowledge.

Slowly they gave back one step and then another. Simsa who watched gathered together all her strength, sent it flowing into those two others. Glorified by the light which was theirs, which they wore like robes of victory, they moved as one, following the retreat of the enemy.

They held no wands, but their arms arose from their sides, with hands outstretched. Fingers moved back and forth, leaving in the air trails of light which shone in the dark with the same radiance as that which cloaked them. Back and forth went those trails, where they touched they held.

There was a flicker of light. The Simsas were no longer facing the enemy, they were behind them. Before the suited men could clumsily wheel about, once more their hands were busy, weaving more streamers of energy which netted. Again they moved so, and again.

Those who had invaded the hall were now within a net wall of shining filaments, criss-crossing, floating up higher than their helmeted heads, enclosing them into a narrow space. They had all fired—first at this portion of the net wall—then at that. The raw energy they unleashed was caught in the spaces between the lines of that net, held there to render their prison stronger, more dangerous—a place for them to die should it grow solid with what they so unleashed in their fear.

They no longer used their weapons. But the fire which the net now restrained was not quenched, it still hung there, holding them. The two Simsas watched for a long moment, as if so they must make sure of their work. Then—

There was no sea now to draw back what had been sent forth. Simsa's own body arched with the sharpness of stabbing pain. She had given birth; now that life must return to her, and its entrance was more agonizing than had been the separation. She gasped, perhaps she voiced a scream. If so she only heard a faint echo of it dying away.

She lay on her back—then there were arms about her, lifting her, holding her as if to assure her safety and peace by firm grasp. She could not lift her hand, her eyelids weighed down to veil her sight. She fought that, looked up to see the blur of Thom's face, his fear for her now easy to read. There was no alien strangeness about him now. She believed that she might reach into his mind if she wished, draw out thoughs he did not even know lay there—though that she would never do.

"It is well." she made her lips shape those words though they seemed stiff and hard to move, as if she had forgotten or not used speech for a long time. "All is well, I think."

He drew her higher in his hold. Her words did not seem

to reassure him. Now she turned her head a little. Had that really happened, had those other parts of her appeared to weave the net of fire? Or had she only dreamed it?

"They—they are caught?" She asked it of him, for in his arms she still was not raised high enough to see the hall below, to know whether she had had some fantastic dream. Once more the balance was swinging—perhaps not so far this time. She could believe it had happened—with another's power.

"Look!" He steadied her with gentle care, drew her still higher, her body yet a limp weight, because she had drawn too heavily upon its resources.

Thus supported she was able to gaze at what was below. Not darkness—there was a splotch of light within the space not far from the outer door. Irregular in shape it was like a great hearth fire burning. From its streams of light rolled slowly upward. She could see no lines of the net, but through the thin wall of the fire itself she sighted the three who had drawn together, facing the wall they could not broach, prisoners of the united powers they had unloosed here.

"I will not ask you how," Thom said slowly, "or what you did. They are caught. Do you know how long it will hold?"

"No." Again that burst of inner knowledge which had led her to this defense was ebbing. It was as if she held a tattered cloak about her, some portions able to give her warmth and covering—rents elsewhere to leave her unprotected. She had been pushed too quickly, too far. There would come a day, of that Simsa was confident, when she could and would command all that had been poured into her through her heritage. But not yet.

"We must go then, while we can. But are you able?" He still held her, though he had gotten to this feet, drawn her up beside him. She discovered that she was able to stand, that the return of those others complete had renewed her strength in part. There was a place where that renewing might become complete.

"The pool," she said. "If I can reach the pool—"

His understanding leaped at once to her meaning. Only the walls, the pit, all which lay between them and that haven . . . . She would need his help to go there. Though she had immobilized these hunters below there were others to come—that she knew. To reach the pool might well be beyond her capability, even with him to aid.

Need could give one strength, Simsa discovered. Somehow she made the descent from the balcony, with her companion beside her on the round of the column, setting her hands to the holds, giving her support again and again.

She was able to stumble along, her stride growing more sure as they left the hall, making a wide circle about those still prisoned. Simsa could see the bubbles of their helmets but not the faces within. Could they be dead? She believed not; their life essence had not withered as the last of their own fire bound them in.

On, Thom's arm around her now and then when she wavered, holding her upright as she paused to gasp, to hold the sceptre close to her body. For it seemed to Simsa that, out of the rod, came more energy. They were fleeing through the deep twilight now. Night had already brought stars into the heavens.

They came to the place of the camp. Others had been before them. Boxes were opened, their contents strewn about. The lamp had been melted down. But Tom still had that light he wore on his belt. He paused long enough to snatch up a bag of provisions—then half carried, half led her on, past the dead—

The journey across the walls taxed Simsa's strength near to the end. When they reached that place where they must go down into the deep rock walled chamber, she wilted to the pavement, knowing that she could not descend on her own power.

Thom dropped the bag beside her, vanished. She was too dazed now to even ask where he would go and why. Then he came back, a coil of thin, tough vine carried like rope across his shoulder. He pulled and twisted with sharp jerks, for testing its strength. Finally he knotted the end about her waist.

"Listen." He had knelt, was looking into her eyes, his hands on her shoulders to hold her steady so that she could not droop away from him, "I shall lower you. Wait there for me—"

Simsa thought she smiled, perhaps her lips did twitch in a weak effort at such. There was nothing else she might do but wait. Did he believe she could go running off now into the dark?

However she did make some shift to help herself by hand and foot holds among the sides of the descent, although she knew that Thom was taking the most of her weight on the taut vine.

Then they were together again, along the passage. When she saw the mists of the pool a last small surge of strength filled her. She pulled away from him, plunged on into that welcome softness which caressed her as if welcoming arms had been opened wide to gather her in, comfort her body, soothe her mind.

Here was the silver sand. Simsa fumbled with the catch of the chain about her hips, let her jeweled kilt fall. Still she took the sceptre with her as she staggered on, dropping at last into the water, as one might fall in exhaustion upon a waiting bed. Around her, supporting her, was that liquid. She lay upon it, her eyes closed.

Sounds, clear, piercing sounds. Those struck sharply into the warm quiet which cradled her. She tried to shut them out, to bar them from this place so that she might not have to answer to them. That they summoned her she dimly knew.

At last she could not deny them. Opening her eyes, Simsa looked up for the second time into the rolling of the mist above the pool. She awakened slowly by degrees, shrinking away somewhat from the shadow of memory —intent on drawing about her only the peace and renewal of this place.

The sounds—

She turned her head, unhappy, uneasy anew.

Near her, their wings outspread upon the water, lying at ease on their backs were the three zorsals. She could no longer wall away memory; had they done what they had been sent to do?

Chirping, she called to them. Zass paddled with all four feet, after flopping over, came to Simsa, resting her head against the girl's shoulder, uttering new cries deep in her long throat.

Shrinkingly, as one might strive to use a limb which had been wounded and might not yet be fully healed, Simsa tried contact by mind with the creature. Again came that twist of alien thought, so difficult to follow. Yet she learned.

It was as if she saw through other eyes, or through a

distance glass such as Thom had, but one which distorted in a manner which made her slightly giddy. There below her (at a different angle and in a fashion which accented things she felt her own eyes might not have seen at all) was that field of wrecked spacers. Things moved there even thought it was half in the shadow. Then there arose a rounded dome of what must have been of the ships. That grew closer and closer, a hole in it larger as she so approached. Within the hole—a broad beam of some kind immediately below. Out again fast, fast, into the night—free, free to fly, to be in the air. Joy which was like a shout of triumph. Free to fly, free, free!

Zass's joy at her healing, her being once more able to live in her own element. But that ship, the beam within—surely they had meant that the zorsals had planted the signal—the signal which might or might not be answered.

Simsa lifted her head. Her dreamy content fled, awareness that they had in no way resolved this venture, crowded in.

No, he had not left her this time. He had been also in the pool. His body, so white against the silver of the sand, was bare of clothing. His head rested on his arm, was turned away. She thought that he must be asleep.

Reluctantly she drew herself back up on the sand. There, coiled in a small shining heap was the girdle of Simsa. The girl reached for it, the links tinkling musically against one another with a small sound of bell notes. She had laid the sceptre across one knee as she locked the chain once more in place, moving slowly because her body's awakening did not seem to keep pace with that of her mind. She felt physically languorous, unwilling to set her hand to anything.

Zass had followed her out of the pool, now squatted down at her side one small forepaw cool against the skin of the girl's thigh as the zorsal looked into her face. Simsa sensed a need for praise, for reassurance that all had been done well. She caught Zass up, held her closely, crooning, rubbed the small head behind the half unrolled antennae. The big eyes were near shut as Zass gurgled in vast contentment.

"They are back."

Simsa was startled, looked around. Thom had rolled over. His head was now chin supported on arms he had folded before him.

"Yes, they are back, and I think that they have done this—" Simsa reported which she had learned from Zass's erratically contacted mind.

Then she had a question of her own: "If the signal has been planted and its message goes forth, when will your ship come? In time?"

"Let us hope so." The serenity which had been on his face when she had looked at him first was replaced by a frown. "But it is as fortune sends."

As fortune sends. The old, old words of the Burrowers by which she had always lived. One could give fortune a nudge now and then as they had tried to do. It remained to be seen how well. While—what did they themselves now face?

He was gazing at her as if she now were as alien to him as the zorsals' minds had been to her.

"What did you do, back there?"

What was the truth? That she did not know. She had wrought with tools she did not understand, to produce something which she could not explain. Still she must make him some answer. There would be many such demands upon her now, she knew—and what answers?

Slowly, fingering the sceptre, looking more often at it than at him. (Why? Because she was suddenly so lonely, knowing that nowhere, even among the far stars now, would she find one who could understand what she saw?) Simsa told him of that strange birth of her other selves, of how they did, not what she had ordered, but what they themselves found necessary for her continued safe existence.

When she had finished there was silence, and that silence lengthened. At first she had not wanted to look at him and see, perhaps, a shadow of disbelief on his face. Then, because of this continued quiet, she did not want to view what was worse—the agreement that she was alien, past contact with those of this age and time.

At last, refusing to surrender to the fact that she might be that indeed, that she was to be likened to one of the stone people of this city come to life, she made herself raise her eyes.

There was wonder in his expression. No—she wanted none of that from anyone, especially him. He had his mysteries brought from the stars, things which would make any of Kuxortal look upon him as greater than life. Was what she did any different in its way? There had been a people once who had mastered other forms of existence, who did not have boxes, and rod weapons, and ships, but held within themselves their own kind of knowledge to build in another way. It was how one used one's inner strengths and how one lived which must be the test of one's knowledge.

Once more she began to speak, not slowly now, because she did not have to seek for words to describe things which were strange and dangerous, and very new to her also. No, this was in a way a plea. She who had never allowed herself to ask, even of Ferwar, what she wanted most—to find another who would be close enough to care where one walked, how one fared in the world.

"You have your nullifiers," she found her tone sharp, challenging, but she did not abate that note—let him believe indeed that she was questioning his way of life against this of her own—"all those death dealers out there!" She pointed to the mist still swirling hypnotically about them.

"You have also spoken of 'talents', of minds which can meet minds, of other wonders. There are many worlds, many peoples, are there not? Both young and old. All have their triumphs and their failures. I do not know why I was born able to take that from what was stored here this knowledge. I do well believe that this may come to be a very heavy burden, one I would willingly pass on to others, if I could. But can you give your hands, your brain, that which is the very essence of you to anyone else?

"There are mysteries past solving. Is that not so? Did you not speak of how bits and pieces of those mysteries are carefully garnered and stored, studied? Did you not tell me of a race which is very old by your toll of seasons, which is also the guardian, the interpreter, of what can so be learned?

"Your brother came here seeking answers. He found puzzles. Some of them were only planted in greed and hate and were of your own time and the devising of your kind. But also he found Simsa.

"And because of that—I am. In Kuxortal I was one who was like an unripened seed which would never have borne fruit. But chance, and you, brought me here. I found my soil, I was planted. I am now what that fortune which men seek, and sometimes fear very much, has made."

"I do not know yet what I can do. Great fear back in that hall forced me into action which was not planned by my mind. It may be that intentions and will and knowledge can live for ages upon ages — be given freely to one who is open to them. I only know that I am not she who you found in Kuxortal. Nor am I wholly she who resigned herself to waiting here. I am more than one, less than the other, but I am person who is real and truly of herself. Though I am not sure as yet what I may be.

"You are of the stars. You have seen many worlds. I know that the race of Simsa was once also of the stars. Though of those I have been left few memories. She remained here. Again I do not know why. Perhaps her star ship could fly no more, perhaps she grew tired of much traveling and wanted only peace. I," she lifted her hands, smoothed back her damp hair, "have only scattered memories and it distresses me — no, it is really painful to draw them back. I want no other life, only that which is now before me."

Then she smiled, a little sadly and added:

"If indeed we have any long life ahead of us. For if your ship does not come, and these who burrow here, even as those other scavengers in the holes of Kuxortal, have their way I do not see much ahead of us now."

He sat up straightly, tossed back that black hair which had grown since he had come planetside. There was no longer that awe — if it had been awe which she had shrunk from recognizing — in his face. She could see his chest arch as he drew a deep breath.

"I do not know either, my lady, who or what you may be. But that you are a wonder for which many men have sought for a long time and never hoped to find. That is plain. We have hunted the Forerunners ever since our first ship landed to view ruins which were strange and empty. They are legends—so old, that even before my race ventured into space there were tales on Arth of earlier visits from aliens who traveled from far stars. That symbol—" he pointed to the horns and ball, "is known to us. We had priestesses in our own dim, long past history who wore such in honor of a goddess who was many things—dear companion to men, tender of the growing food, cherisher of children—and ready in her wrath to strike down those who threatened all such. Perhaps there was a Simsa there once. She was remembered for long and long.

"But here you have accepted from the past what we have longed to know."

Simsa shook her head. "No, I shall not be another treasure for your people to hold. I am alive, a person, not an ancient carving, a handful of jewels set into some alien pattern."

She pointed to the cuff still about his forearm. Though he had shed all else of his clothing to bathe in the pool, still that was snugly fitted to him.

"Why did you not take that off?" she asked. "Do you expect still another attack?"

He glanced down as if a little surprised that he still wore it. Then his fingers fumbled, he turned it about and about, but the band would not slide from his forearm. It was not tight enough to pinch the flesh, neither would the cuff give enough for him to rid himself of it, in spite of his efforts, which she watched quietly until she said:

"It would seem that you, too, will carry a portion of the past with you. What will you do when you reach your home place? Cut off your hand that your kind may have what you wear to puzzle over? A lost hand, a lost freedom, neither will serve us. I shall perhaps talk to your seekers of learning, in my own time and place—if we ever leave this world. But I am to be no prisoner of theirs because they think me some 'treasure'!"

"They will not." He said that quietly, but in his eyes there was a stronger promise. How well he might keep that promise she could not tell. That, like all else, must be answered by time itself.

Suddenly she laughed. "We speak as two who have the good will of fortune, we who are not even sure we shall be alive with tomorrow's sun."

He did not look dismayed. Instead he stretched wide his arms, as one who awakens from a refreshing sleep to face the brightest of good days on a morning at the first of the dry-season.

"I shall swear by fortune, Lady Simsa, who is herself and no other, that is what I believe. We shall live—and we shall seek the stars in freedom."

Now Simsa again smiled in return. She also nursed a promising lightness of spirit. Perhaps it was the influence of the pool's renewing, perhaps it was something else—his promise? Or maybe—she shied away from following that thought any farther now. She must learn herself before she strove to teach others, especially this man from the stars to which Simsa would return. *Yes!* That she too believed now, even as she believed in the realness of the sand about her, the shining of the pool, the heaviness of the ring about her thumb—that a new day would come tomorrow!

THE END

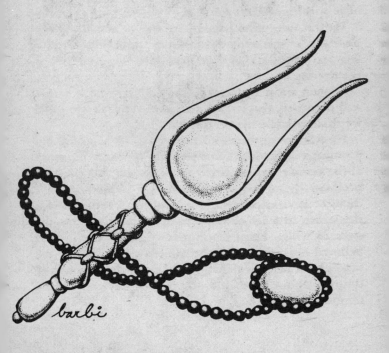

barbi

barbi

ATTENTION: SCHOOLS AND CORPORATIONS

PINNACLE Books are available at quantity discounts with bulk purchases for educational, business or special promotional use. For further details, please write to: SPECIAL SALES MANAGER, Pinnacle Books, Inc., 271 Madison Ave., Suite 904, New York, NY 10016.

WRITE FOR OUR FREE CATALOG

If there is a Pinnacle Book you want—and you cannot find it locally—it is available from us simply by sending the title and price plus 75¢ to cover mailing and handling costs to:

Pinnacle Books, Inc.
Reader Service Department
1430 Broadway
New York, NY 10018

Please allow 6 weeks for delivery.

☐ Check here if you want to receive our catalog regularly.